STAR WARS

THE CLONE WARS

Warriors of the Deep

STAR WARS®

THE CLONE WARS™

Warriors of the Deep
adapted by Rob Valois

Grosset & Dunlap
An Imprint of Penguin Group (USA) Inc.
LucasBooks

GROSSET & DUNLAP
Published by the Penguin Group
Penguin Group (USA) Inc., 375 Hudson Street, New York, New York 10014, USA
Penguin Group (Canada), 90 Eglinton Avenue East, Suite 700,
Toronto, Ontario M4P 2Y3, Canada
(a division of Pearson Penguin Canada Inc.)
Penguin Books Ltd., 80 Strand, London WC2R 0RL, England
Penguin Group Ireland, 25 St. Stephen's Green, Dublin 2, Ireland
(a division of Penguin Books Ltd.)
Penguin Group (Australia), 250 Camberwell Road, Camberwell, Victoria 3124,
Australia (a division of Pearson Australia Group Pty. Ltd.)
Penguin Books India Pvt. Ltd., 11 Community Centre,
Panchsheel Park, New Delhi—110 017, India
Penguin Group (NZ), 67 Apollo Drive, Rosedale, Auckland 0632, New Zealand
(a division of Pearson New Zealand Ltd.)
Penguin Books (South Africa) (Pty.) Ltd., 24 Sturdee Avenue,
Rosebank, Johannesburg 2196, South Africa

Penguin Books Ltd., Registered Offices:
80 Strand, London WC2R 0RL, England

This book is published in partnership with LucasBooks, a division of Lucasfilm Ltd.

Copyright © 2011 Lucasfilm Ltd. & ® or ™ where indicated. All Rights Reserved.
Used Under Authorization. Published by Grosset & Dunlap, a division of
Penguin Young Readers Group, 345 Hudson Street, New York, New York 10014.
GROSSET & DUNLAP is a trademark of Penguin Group (USA) Inc.
Printed in the U.S.A.

ISBN 978-0-448-45727-7   10 9 8 7 6 5 4 3 2 1

On the bridge of a Republic cruiser floating above the frozen world of Iceberg III in the Calamari system, Jedi Master Plo Koon stood before a hologram of Jedi Master Yoda.

"Troubling this news is," Yoda said. "The Calamari system is crucial to the stability of the Republic."

"We were able to prevent General Grievous from invading the system," Plo Koon reported. "Our forces defeated him here at Iceberg III, and his ships seem to have been driven from the area."

"Responsible the Separatists were for the murder of King Kolina?" Yoda asked.

"There's no evidence to support that they were involved," Plo Koon replied. "However, King Kolina was the only thing keeping the peace between the

Mon Calamari and the Quarren. If Mon Cala falls into Separatist hands, we not only lose an important ally, but we also lose access to their ore mines."

"Critical to our fleet's defenses the Mon Cala ore is," Yoda added. "Into the Separatist's hands it must not fall."

"The Mon Calamari and the Quarren council are holding an emergency session to choose a new leader," Plo Koon said.

"Send someone to mediate, we must," Yoda said. "Senator Amidala to Mon Cala will go."

CHAPTER ONE

Deep in the Outer Rim Territories sat the world of Mon Cala, a water world not far from the ice planet of Iceberg III. This bluish-white planet was home to several species of aquatic life, mainly the warlike Quarren and their peace-loving neighbors, the Mon Calamari.

The Mon Calamari were fishlike in appearance. They had humanoid bodies with salmon-colored skin, webbed hands, and high-domed heads. They also had huge, fishlike eyes that could move around independently from each other, allowing them to look in two directions at once. They could breathe just as easily out of water as they could in it.

The Quarren were also humanoids, but with large, squidlike heads that had multiple tentacles that hung from their faces. Unlike the Mon Calamari, the

Quarren had small mouths with two fanglike teeth on either side and a long, thin tongue that stuck out in between.

The Mon Calamari and Quarren lived separately in massive underwater cities constructed among the coral and rock that rose from the deep seafloor.

The two races had always struggled to maintain a peaceful coexistence, but as the Clone Wars escalated throughout the galaxy, the Mon Calamari and Quarren soon found themselves on different ends of the political landscape.

Under King Yos Kolina, Mon Cala—the Mon Calamari and Quarren—had long been united in its support of the Galactic Republic and the Jedi.

But when King Kolina was found mysteriously murdered, the Quarren seized the opportunity to break free from Mon Calamari rule and demanded their own Quarren leader.

The Mon Calamari rejected their claims and insisted that the King's young son, Prince Lee-Char, become instated as the rightful King of all Mon Cala.

The Separatist Alliance was a group of worlds who rejected Republic rule. Led by the sinister Count Dooku, its power and influence spread throughout the galaxy.

Its goal was to destroy the Galactic Republic and the Jedi Order who served as protectors of the Republic. The Separatists had been secretly infiltrating Republic worlds and manipulating the governments to turn them to their side of the war.

Since the death of King Kolina, the leaders of the Galactic Republic worried that Mon Cala might fall under the influence of the Separatists.

An emergency gathering of the Mon Calamari and Quarren leaders had been called to discuss the future of Mon Cala. Fearing that the Quarren would not acknowledge Prince Lee-Char as the rightful King of Mon Cala, the Mon Calamari requested that the Republic Senate intervene on their behalf.

While it was the Republic Senate's policy not to assert themselves into the internal politics of any world, they did offer to send the Galactic Senator from the nearby planet of Naboo, Padmé Amidala, to observe and, if needed, offer advice. Accompanying her was Jedi Knight Anakin Skywalker.

Padmé Amidala was a young but highly respected member of the Galactic Senate. As a Senator, it was her duty to help mediate disputes among the worlds of the Republic.

After arriving on Mon Cala, Padmé and Anakin traveled deep underwater to the legislative chambers in Mon Calamari City. Protected by deep-sea scuba gear that allowed them to breathe, Padmé and Anakin watched as the giant hall filled with Mon Calamari and Quarren delegates.

Before the official talks had even begun, they could sense the tension in the room. "The Mon Calamari and Quarren are hardly even speaking to one another," Padmé said.

"Or if they are, it's not to say anything particularly nice," Anakin added.

"I don't understand how things could have gotten so bad so quickly," Padmé said. "The Quarren and Mon Calamari have always squabbled, but this seems like so much more."

Across the hall, Anakin watched as a mighty, sharklike Karkarodon swam through the crowd.

The Karkarodons were humanoid creatures from the planet Karkaris—a water world that resided in a system not far from Mon Cala. They had massive jaws, razor-sharp teeth, and were fearless warriors. Anakin recognized the Karkarodon as Separatist Commander Riff Tamson.

"He must be here as an ambassador of Count

Dooku," Anakin said. "I think I'm starting to understand what's going on here. And I don't like the looks of it."

Anakin watched as Tamson swam behind the Quarren delegation. "I'm going to keep my eye on him," Anakin said. "If Dooku sent one of his commanders, I'm guessing his army isn't too far behind."

"Remember that we're on a diplomatic mission, Anakin," Padmé said. "Just because the Separatists sent an ambassador doesn't mean that you need to start blowing things up."

With Tamson's arrival, the Quarren grew more aggressive and defiant. "The rule of the Mon Calamari must come to an end," one of the Quarren leaders announced.

"You've all prospered under our rule," a Mon Calamari delegate replied.

"But now that rule has ended," a Quarren delegate added. "It's time for a change!"

The room started to drift into anarchy. Delegates from both sides began shouting. "The Prince's rule has been preordained!" a Mon Calamari voice called out.

"Down with the monarchy!" several Quarren yelled out.

"We'll defend our right for a Mon Calamari King!" a voice shot back.

The Quarren voices continued. "We want a Quarren King! Down with the Mon Calamari! Power to the Quarren!"

Anakin and Padmé exchanged concerned looks. There didn't seem like much chance that the Mon Calamari and Quarren would ever come to an agreement.

Then young Prince Lee-Char rose and tried to calm the crowd. "I am dedicated to serving the Quarren as well as my own people, the Mon Calamari," he said.

For a moment, everyone in the room stopped arguing and all eyes were focused on the Prince.

"Silence!" Riff Tamson called from the back. He swam up toward the Prince. "You haven't earned the right to speak at this gathering!"

The Prince, who was no more than a child, retreated. He was intimidated by the Separatist commander.

A Mon Calamari soldier dove forward, blocking the Karkarodon. "You have no say in this matter, ambassador," Captain Ackbar said. "You are only here as an observer for the Separatists."

Tamson turned to face the Mon Calamari. "Do not forget I am here at the request of the Quarren because *you*, Captain, demanded the presence of the Republic."

Enraged, Ackbar moved in closer to the Separatist commander. Before the Mon Calamari captain could reach his target, Anakin swam in and restrained him.

Padmé watched as Nossor Ri, the leader of the Quarren, made his way over to them.

"Prince Lee-Char has neither the experience nor the knowledge to lead," he said, gesturing to the young Mon Calamari. "The boy will bring the planet to ruin."

"Please," Padmé pleaded to Nossor Ri. "You came here today in hopes of finding a compromise. I still believe one can be achieved. Tell me, what can the Republic do to help keep the peace?"

"The Republic has no place here," Nossor Ri replied. "This matter is between the Quarren and the Mon Calamari. And the Quarren refuse to support the coronation of another Mon Calamari King. I'm sorry."

"But you have to understand—" Padmé began before Tamson cut her off.

"It is my opinion that the Quarren have no further business here," Tamson said before turning to swim off.

The Quarren delegates began to exit the hall, leaving the Mon Calamari to ponder what would come next.

Anakin turned to Captain Ackbar. "Come on, Captain, we have to contact Master Yoda. With the Separatists involved, I have a feeling that this will not end peacefully."

After everyone had left the hall, Prince Lee-Char sat down and hung his head.

A hand landed on Lee-Char's shoulder. The Prince slowly picked up his head and saw Nossor Ri standing over him.

"Your father was my trusted friend," Nossor Ri said. "I am sorry for your loss."

Lee-Char and Nossor exchanged a solemn look before the Quarren swam off.

CHAPTER TWO

A Republic frigate floated in the space above Mon Cala. Aboard the ship, Anakin, Padmé, and Captain Ackbar addressed holograms of Jedi Masters Yoda and Mace Windu.

The Jedi had long been peacekeepers throughout the galaxy. Their role had always been to advise and protect.

With the rise of the Clone Wars, the Jedi had assumed the roles of military leaders. The Jedi Council, which was based on the planet Coruscant, commanded the Republic's massive army of clone troopers.

The head of the council was the wise Master Yoda. Together, he and Mace Windu oversaw all the Republic's military operations via hologram from the halls of the Jedi Council.

The Jedi Masters listened quietly as Anakin reported the outcome of the meeting between the Quarren and Mon Calamari.

"Hmm . . . ," Yoda said. "This civil war, is it inevitable?"

"Sadly so, Master Yoda," Captain Ackbar replied.

"The Separatists sent an ambassador to stir up the Quarren, and that's exactly what he did," Anakin added. "There was no reasoning with any of the Quarren delegates."

Finally, Senator Amidala addressed the Jedi.

"It's only a matter of time before the Quarren withdraw from the Republic," she said. "We must do something to prevent this from happening. Too many worlds have already abandoned the Republic."

"Troubling times these are." Yoda nodded in agreement. "Behind this I suspect Count Dooku is."

"The Mon Calamari system is still part of the Republic," Mace Windu added. "This planet must not fall into Separatist hands. I'll dispatch Master Fisto and your Padawan, Tano, along with a company of clones. They'll be at your side by day's end. In the meantime, Captain, assemble the Mon Calamari troops and prepare for a Quarren assault."

The underwater city of Mon Calamari was bustling with activity when Captain Ackbar arrived. News of the impending civil war had spread quickly through the city.

As he hurtled along inside one of the many clear transport tubes that connected the city's buildings, Ackbar watched people rush about to collect whatever food and supplies they could gather. Soon, he feared mobs and rioting would break out across the city. As he approached the royal residence, Captain Ackbar saw Mon Calamari guards escorting Prince Lee-Char and Senator Meena Tills to a secure balcony.

The young Prince looked out over the city in chaos. He struggled to make sense of it all. With his father gone, the people of Mon Cala had lost hope. He felt like there was nothing that he could possibly do to help his people. Without a word, Senator Tills came over and turned him away from the crazed scene below the palace.

Captain Ackbar waited at attention for the Prince to greet him.

"Captain, please give us an update on the status of the military," the Senator asked as she stood protectively next to the Prince.

"The troops are being assembled, Senator," Ackbar reported. "The city guard has already mobilized, and I expect to have all reserve forces activated by the end of the day."

"Let's hope we don't need them, Captain," the Mon Calamari Senator replied.

"Agreed," Ackbar replied, although he was sure that his people would soon be at war.

"Captain, I have something very important that I need you to do," the Senator added. "I'm entrusting the safety of Prince Lee-Char to your hands. You must remain at his side at all times as his personal bodyguard."

Captain Ackbar was unsure how to respond to the Senator. He was a soldier, not a bodyguard. His place was on the front lines, protecting the Mon Calamari people.

"Senator, if the boy is to—" Ackbar began to reply, but the Senator cut him off.

"We are on the verge of a civil war," she said. "And that boy is the supreme commander of the Mon Calamari's military. It's up to *you* to see that he remains safe and that he can handle the job."

"With all due respect, Senator," Ackbar said, looking to the young boy standing next to him, "the Prince is not ready to lead an army. He needs training."

"You have your orders, Captain." With that, Senator Tills turned and swam off.

The captain looked at the young boy, unsure of how to handle this assignment.

The Prince looked back at Ackbar. "You are right, Captain. I am not trained to lead an army. I am in no position to lead our people."

It pained Ackbar to hear the Prince say those words. Lee-Char was the future King of the Mon Calamari. It was Captain Ackbar's duty to prepare the young Prince for his role as the ruler of Mon Cala.

"Come on, Your Highness," Ackbar said to Lee-Char. "We have a war to win."

Deep underwater sat Quarren City. It was a dark and foreboding place that few Mon Calamari visited.

The Quarren preferred the dark corners and winding caves of the seafloor. Above the tall buildings that spiraled out of the coral, squads of Separatist aqua droids swam past several giant, squidlike Trident drill ships.

The Trident drill ships were stealthy, underwater assault crafts that moved through the water like an octopus or squid with their tentaclelike legs propelling them along. The ships also carried many legions of deadly aqua droids.

The aqua droids resembled the B2 super battle droids, but were sleeker and designed for aquatic combat. They were armed with retractable laser cannons, and their feet could transform into propellers that moved them along at great speeds.

Aboard the Trident command ship, Riff Tamson stood before a hologram of Separatist leader Count Dooku.

Dooku had once been a Jedi Master before succumbing to the dark side and abandoning the order. He soon became one of the most ruthless adversaries the Jedi had faced.

"The army has assembled," Tamson reported to Dooku.

"Well done, Tamson. What about the Quarren leader?" Dooku asked.

"The Quarren leader is on board with our plan one hundred percent," Tamson replied. "He will deliver the planet into your hands just as you said he would."

Count Dooku nodded. "Very good, Commander. In the end, this planet will be under your control. Proceed as planned."

Groups of concerned Mon Calamari officials gathered in the capital city. In his father's throne room, Prince Lee-Char stood in front of the riotous crowd. Senator Tills and Captain Ackbar took their places beside the Prince while Anakin and Padmé watched from the wings.

The Prince nervously swam forward to address the Mon Calamari Assembly.

"I know many of you agree with the Quarren. You agree that I am too young to rule," Lee-Char began. "But I assure you I will use all my strength and all my abilities to lead us through this challenge. We are a great people, and I will do all I can to negotiate peace without bloodshed. There is no reason to believe that the Quarren will attack."

The crowd quieted while listening to their Prince. They needed to believe that there would be peace.

Suddenly, an explosion rocked the throne room. Captain Ackbar moved quickly to the window. Outside, he saw aqua droids and Trident drill ships descending on the city.

"It's an attack!" he called as he made his way back to the Prince. Padmé and Anakin were already by Lee-Char's side when he returned.

"Come on, Your Highness," Ackbar said. "We've got to get you to safety."

Debris rained down as Ackbar and Padmé escorted the Prince to the nearest exit. Anakin ignited his lightsaber and deflected the rubble as it came toward them.

Once outside the chamber, they watched the Mon Calamari Army mobilizing. The soldiers had been caught off guard and were struggling to create a defensive barrier around the city.

Ackbar knew that the Quarren were coming for the Prince. He had to keep him safe.

CHAPTER THREE

Explosions raged across the city. Quarren soldiers riding minisubs that resembled underwater speeder bikes tore through the maze of city buildings while squads of aqua droids made their way through the city streets. It was a full-on invasion.

"Captain, we need to get the Prince and the Senator to safety," Anakin said as he and Captain Ackbar led Padmé and Prince Lee-Char from the throne room and out into the city. "Out here in the open we're defenseless."

"The city guard should have set up a perimeter around the city center," Captain Ackbar replied. "That's our best option."

"You've got the lead, Captain," Anakin said. "I'll stick back and keep an eye on the Prince and Senator Amidala. If we're quick, we should be fine."

They moved through the smoke-filled water until Captain Ackbar spotted a squad of Mon Calamari soldiers holding a defensive position in the city's main square.

"All right," Ackbar said as he raised his hand to hold up the others. "We just need to make it across to the main square. We'll be out in the open, but if we hustle, we should be fine."

"Your Highness," Anakin said to the Prince. "I'm going to need you to stay low. Once we start, don't stop until we've made it to the other side."

Prince Lee-Char nodded in understanding. As soon as Ackbar gave the word, they moved out into the open.

Aqua droid blaster fire was instantly upon them. Anakin ignited his lightsaber and deflected the incoming blasts as Captain Ackbar returned fire.

Padmé could feel the Prince slowing down with every blast that tore past them. "Come on, Prince. We've got to keep moving," she said as she ushered him along behind Anakin and Captain Ackbar. "We're almost there."

As they approached the city square, the Mon Calamari soldiers turned to watch. For many, this was the first time they'd ever seen a Jedi. Then one of the soldiers noticed the Prince swimming up behind Captain Ackbar.

"The Prince! The Prince is here!" the soldier cheered. "He's joining the battle."

Soon, the other soldiers rushed the Prince to safety behind the front lines.

The Mon Calamari commander swam over to them. He paused in front of the Prince, awaiting his orders. All eyes were on Lee-Char, who was overwhelmed by the battle unfolding around him.

Ackbar moved in next to the Prince. "What are your orders, Your Highness?" he asked.

The Prince looked to Ackbar and then to the commander. He wondered what his father, the King, would have said in this situation. King Yos Kolina was a strong, confident leader who had led both the Mon Calamari and Quarren soldiers into many battles.

As a young child, Lee-Char had heard many tales of his father's bravery. The young boy had wanted nothing more than to grow up and become a leader like his father.

Lee-Char knew exactly what he must do. He took a deep breath and addressed the two officers. "Stay where you are and hold the line," he said.

The Quarren forces were overtaking Mon Calamari City. Anakin could see that the Mon Calamari were outgunned and that they wouldn't be able to hold off the assault for long. He didn't want to be disrespectful to Captain Ackbar and the other Mon Calamari, but the Prince was just an inexperienced boy. He had no idea how to lead an army, and Anakin feared he would send his people to their deaths.

"If I may suggest, Captain," he said. "We should take the Prince to a safer place until the Republic reinforcements arrive."

Ackbar stood strong against the Jedi. "No. That is a decision only the Prince can make," he said. "He is our leader."

Anakin respected Captain Ackbar. He was a brave soldier and a wise commander. He also knew that the future of Mon Cala rested on the shoulders of Prince Lee-Char—and that the Mon Calamari people needed to be able to look upon him as their leader. But none of that would do any good if they were all destroyed by the Quarren assault.

All around the city square, Mon Calamari soldiers were being knocked back by Quarren blaster fire. The Prince looked at his fallen men.

"This is horrible!" Prince Lee-Char cried. He was responsible for their lives, and he had ordered them to hold the line.

Anakin tried to plead with the Prince. "Your Highness," he said. "Holding this position is not a wise decision. We have to get you to safety."

Then the Jedi looked to Ackbar. "And you know it. Forget your tradition. This is war!"

All eyes were on Lee-Char. The young Prince choked on his words.

Part of him wanted to run back to the palace and hide away until it was all over. But what if he did run? What would the others think of their Prince? Would they stay and fight, or would they run, too? He had to lead by example. He had to stay and fight.

"Your Majesty?" Ackbar said, trying to get an answer out of his Prince.

After a beat, Lee-Char looked up at Ackbar. "I have to stay here with my people. Press your attack, Captain."

Ackbar wasted no time. He drew his blaster and charged to the front line. Around him, all he could hear was the sound of blaster fire. Through the smoky water, he saw the two sides engaged in a massive battle.

Tamson came tearing through the water. His mighty jaws viciously bit and tore through several Mon Calamari troops.

The troops were scattered and disorganized. The overwhelming Quarren forces had shaken their courage. Ackbar swam into the heart of the battle. "Soldiers of Mon Calamari," he called out. "This is your home. Do not let it fall!"

The soldiers cheered and rallied behind Captain Ackbar. As a unit, they charged into battle against squads of aqua droids.

Seeing this, the Prince turned to Anakin and Padmé. "I need to get some troops behind those Separatist droids. That's the only chance they have."

Without giving Padmé and Anakin a chance to respond, Prince Lee-Char swam off. "Come on," he called back to them. "I know a shortcut."

Anakin and Padmé chased behind him with a small team of Mon Calamari soldiers. They followed him through a maze of transport tubes.

"We should come out right behind them," the Prince called back to Anakin.

Just then, an explosion ripped through the transport tube, blocking their way.

"What do we do now?" Padmé asked.

"Well, we've got to come up with another plan," Anakin replied. Then he looked at the Prince. "Any ideas?" he asked.

"Our only hope now is to wait for the Jedi reinforcements to arrive," the Prince replied.

Above the surface of Mon Cala, three Republic gunships moved into position over the water. "Blue Leader standing by," Padawan Ahsoka Tano reported into her comlink as she and a team of scuba clones prepared to jump into the deep, alien waters.

The Togruta Jedi and her clones stood ready in their scuba gear as the other units reported in. "Red Leader standing by," came clone Commander Monnk. Then she heard Captain Rex reporting from the Jedi cruiser.

"All squadrons are in position, General Fisto," Rex reported to the team leader. "You may deploy when ready."

From the third gunship, Jedi Master Kit Fisto stood with his squad of scuba clones. The Nautolan wore no scuba gear. He was from the planet Glee Anselm, a water world in the Mid Rim, and was able to breathe underwater as freely as the Mon Calamari or Quarren. Kit Fisto had greenish skin, large, dark eyes, and long head-tresses that fell down below his shoulders. He spoke into his comlink. "Commencing deployment now, three . . . two . . . one . . . mark!"

On his command, he, the scuba clones, Ahsoka, and Commander Monnk descended into the depths of the Mon Cala ocean and prepared for battle.

CHAPTER FOUR

With all paths of escape blocked, Anakin, the
Prince, and Padmé rejoined the main battle. It was
a grim scene. Quarren forces had advanced on the
Mon Calamari soldiers, who struggled to hold them
off. It seemed that there was little hope that the Mon
Calamari would be able to defend their city.

Moving through the water above the battle,
Anakin saw the Republic troops come into sight.
"Reinforcements!" he called to the others. "Finally!"

Leading the assault was Kit Fisto. He piloted a
handheld Republic propulsion sub into the heart of
the battle. Behind him came Commander Monnk
and the scuba clones. The scuba clone armor was a
lightweight version of the traditional clone armor
and had aquatic propulsion packs installed on the
back that allowed the clones to maneuver through

the water quickly. They carried modified blasters which allowed the weapons to fire underwater.

"Red Team, move into position," Commander Monnk ordered his men. "Let's drive these Quarren soldiers back down to the bottom of the ocean."

"Roger that," a scuba clone replied as Red Team opened fire on the Quarren soldiers.

The Quarren Army wasn't prepared for a Republic assault. They dropped back behind the aqua droids as the clone army descended upon them.

"And we'll take care of those aqua droids," Kit Fisto added. He piloted his sub directly into the heart of the droid army. Once close enough, he pushed off from the sub and ignited his lightsaber.

Maneuvering easily through the water, the Nautolan Jedi began to slice through the oncoming aqua droids as his team of scuba clones moved in behind him.

"Let's teach these deep-sea clankers a thing or two about underwater combat," a scuba clone sergeant called to the others. With precision shots, the clones blasted at the droids.

The Republic forces quickly took control of the situation. The Mon Calamari soldiers rallied behind them, and for the first time since the battle began they felt that they were able to defend their home.

As the offensive slowed, Padmé pulled back from the main battle and called to Anakin. "I'm going to look for Senator Tills," she said. "Hopefully she's still alive."

No one had seen Senator Tills since all the Mon Calamari had fled the throne room during the attack.

"Be careful!" Anakin called to Padmé as she swam off. He didn't feel comfortable letting her go off on her own, especially in a war zone.

Just then, Prince Lee-Char yelled, "Look out!"

An aqua droid came up quickly behind Anakin. The Jedi spun around and cut down the droid before it could strike.

With the Republic forces now in the fight, the battle for Mon Cala became an all-out war. Anakin could no longer stay on the sidelines and protect the Prince. He needed to help lead the Republic forces.

He swam to Lee-Char. "Stay down and don't move," he told the Prince as he ignited his lightsaber and swam off into battle.

Seeing Anakin enter the battle, Ackbar quickly moved back to defend the Prince. Lee-Char could hear the soldiers cheering in the distance.

"Do you hear that?" Ackbar asked. "They're cheering for you."

"They're cheering for them," Prince Lee-Char said as he pointed at the Republic forces.

"Then make it for you," Ackbar replied as he handed Lee-Char a blaster. "Come on. Lead."

Ackbar swam back to the battle, leaving Lee-Char to ponder his words.

Anakin swam deeper into the escalating battle. The Quarren soldiers were well-trained and were beginning to overwhelm the Mon Calamari defenders.

A group of Quarren surrounded Anakin. The Jedi swung his lightsaber through the water as they charged him.

One of the Quarren grabbed Anakin from behind and wrapped one of its long, clawed hands around his scuba helmet. Anakin struggled to break free, but his attacker was more skilled at underwater combat. Using all his strength, the Jedi pushed free, but his helmet became dislodged. There was no way for Anakin to breathe.

Anakin continued fighting as he struggled to hold his breath. He knew that he couldn't hold out too long and that he'd have to find his helmet. He was far too deep in the ocean to swim to the surface, and there were too many Quarren soldiers blocking his way.

He focused his energy and sliced through the Quarren soldiers. His eyes searched the water for his scuba helmet, and then he saw the aqua droids coming at him.

Anakin concentrated on the Force and made one last attempt to fend off his attackers. Just as he was about to run out of breath, blaster fire tore through the droids. Then a familiar figure came into sight. It was his Padawan, Ahsoka Tano.

"You called for backup?" she asked with a smile as she slowed down her handheld propulsion sub and handed him his helmet.

Anakin put the helmet on and vacated the water from the airtight chamber. He took a deep breath and then looked at his pupil. "I had . . . it under control . . . Snips."

"Ha!" She laughed at her Master. "I knew you'd say that."

Ahsoka turned and headed back toward the battle. Anakin's comlink went off as he got ready to follow. It was Padmé.

"Anakin, I need you down here," she called out. "It's Senator Tills . . . I need help getting her to safety. We're at the base of the palace. And hurry."

Anakin swam up to Ahsoka. "I need you to cover the Prince. I'm going for the Senators."

Ahsoka turned around and headed for the Prince. "You got it, Master," she replied.

Anakin swam as fast as he could to the base of the palace. There, he saw Padmé, Meena Tills, and two lone Mon Calamari soldiers holding off a squad of Quarren attackers.

He moved in fast behind the Quarren. Before they'd realized what was happening, the Jedi was on top of them.

Once the Quarren soldiers were defeated, Anakin led the Senators back to the Republic base camp.

Ahsoka hurried back to the Prince, who had been left alone on the outskirts of the battlefield. Her minisub tore through the water at top speed.

From the dark, cloudy water a pair of sharklike eyes fixed upon the unprotected Prince. Ahsoka immediately sensed the threat, but before she could react, Tamson was almost upon Lee-Char.

The young Jedi ignited her lightsaber and aimed her minisub at the oncoming Karkarodon.

The sharklike Tamson dodged the attack, but it gave Ahsoka an opportunity to reach the Prince.

"Grab on!" she called to Lee-Char.

"Good idea!" Lee-Char replied as he grabbed hold of Ahsoka's sub. They zipped away with Tamson in hot pursuit. "Get us out of here!"

"Hang on!" Ahsoka yelled as she spun and twisted her sub, trying to avoid Tamson.

"I am! I am!" the Prince replied, struggling to keep his grip on the sub.

Ahsoka continued to maneuver the sub, trying to make it to the safety of the transport tubes.

"Look out!" Lee-Char yelled as he spotted a team of aqua droids. "They're coming right at us."

Behind them, Ahsoka could see Tamson moving in quickly. She had to get rid of the droids if they had any chance of getting away.

"I'm letting go!" Ahsoka yelled as she and Lee-Char released the sub, sending it straight into the droids. The sub exploded on contact, clearing the way for Ahsoka and the Prince.

Tamson charged the tube, ramming it hard.

"As long as we're in the tube, we're safe," Lee-Char told Ahsoka. The two hid in the safety of the tube until a squad of Mon Calamari soldiers arrived.

Finally, with one last burst of speed, Tamson rammed his head through the wall of the tube, his jaws snarling and snapping. The Mon Calamari soldiers fired their blasters at Tamson. Realizing he was overpowered, he abandoned his attack and fled.

CHAPTER FIVE

A Separatist landing craft hovered into position above the vast Mon Cala ocean. The ship's cargo bay doors opened and, one by one, unmarked containers tumbled into the deep.

In the dark recesses of the underwater kelp forest, Nossor Ri and Riff Tamson waited in anticipation of the mysterious Separatist cargo.

Nossor Ri had begun to grow concerned about the Separatist forces and their effectiveness against the Mon Calamari and Republic Army. He'd been promised an elite army to aid the Quarren in assuming power on Mon Cala.

Although they seemed to under perform, Nossor Ri was glad to have the aqua droids on the front lines. He'd rather witness their destruction than the deaths of his Quarren soldiers.

"Your aqua droids are hardly a match for the Republic Army," Nossor Ri said to Riff Tamson. "What makes you think these secret weapons you've brought from your home world will fare any better?"

Tamson smiled a sharp-toothed grin. "These secret weapons are half machine and half monster," he explained. "We call them Hydroid Medusas, and they are invincible."

Nossor Ri watched as cargo containers the size of buildings crashed to the ocean floor. From each emerged a monstrous Hydroid Medusa. These mechanized creatures appeared to be giant, glowing jellyfish with long, electrified tentacles.

Tamson and Nossor Ri inspected the massive, jellyfishlike Hydroid Medusas. The Quarren leader seemed pleased with their new weapons. Power like this is why he chose to side with the Separatists. For generations, the Quarren had lived under a Mon Calamari King. It was now their time to rule, even if it meant aligning with Count Dooku and Separatists like Tamson.

Nossor Ri had been promised that once the Mon Calamari surrendered, the Quarren would be officially instated as the rulers of Mon Cala. He would oversee the rebuilding of the world himself—

it would be the dawn of a new era for the Quarren and Mon Calamari.

After returning the Senators to the safety of the town square, Anakin rejoined Kit Fisto on the front lines.

The battle appeared to be turning in favor of the combined Republic and Mon Calamari forces as the Quarren soldiers and Separatist aqua droids dropped back.

"It appears that they are returning to their ships," Kit Fisto said. "We seem to have won this round."

"We are lucky to have survived the first assault," Captain Ackbar added, swimming up to join them.

Anakin wasn't too sure about their apparent victory. "They could've easily overrun us with their droids," he said.

Kit Fisto seemed in agreement with Anakin. He pulled out his electrobinoculars and took a closer look at the retreating Separatist forces.

"The droids are taking up position in the coral," Master Fisto said. "Probably amassing for another assault."

"Why would they hide in the coral?" Anakin wondered.

"We need to get back to the city," Ackbar said. "There's a lot we need to do before the next attack."

Back in the makeshift base camp in the town square, the Republic and Mon Calamari forces hurried to regroup and organize before the next Quarren assault.

Medical and aid stations were being constructed under the safety of the transport tubes that stretched across the square.

The Prince, seeing the Senators return, rushed to greet them. "Senator Tills, I am glad to see you're safe," he said.

The Senator nodded in response. "I, too, am glad to see you're well," she said. "There is much to be done now that our enemy is on the retreat."

"Preparations are already being made to reinforce the front lines," the Prince said. "And we've set up additional aid stations throughout the city."

Senator Tills ignored his words. "You must prepare to dictate terms for a Quarren surrender," she demanded.

The Prince was shocked by this. The Quarren may have been pushed back, but even he knew that they were far from ready to give up.

Anakin, Kit Fisto, and Captain Ackbar saw the Prince and Senator speaking as they entered the city square.

"What do you think is going on over there?" Anakin asked. "The Prince doesn't seem too happy."

"No, he does not," Ackbar agreed as he swam over toward the Prince. The two Jedi followed behind him. As they got closer, they could make out what the Senator was saying.

"It's your duty as the Prince of Mon Cala—the future King—to demand a Quarren surrender," she said.

"Not so fast, Senator," Ackbar added. "I don't think we're in any position to make demands of the Quarren. They are not going to surrender that easily."

"I agree with Captain Ackbar," Lee-Char said. "I know the Quarren. They won't surrender."

Anakin swam forward. "We may have won the first battle," he said. "But it won't be the last."

"It's only a matter of time before the Quarren launch another assault, Senator," Ackbar added. "We need to make sure the military is ready for a second attack. I don't want to be caught off guard again."

Inside his helmet, Anakin took a deep breath. For an instant, he seemed somewhere else. "I sense the real battle is about to begin," he said.

With that, they heard a low grumbling sound and looked to see the approaching Hydroid Medusas. The giant jellyfish creatures illuminated the ocean around them as their electrified tentacles crackled through the water.

Prince Lee-Char stood in shock. "We have no defense against those!"

Anakin ignited his lightsaber and headed toward the Medusas. "This isn't going to be easy," he said.

"Come with me, Prince," Senator Tills said. "We need to get you to safety."

The Prince looked to Ackbar who was gearing up to enter the battle.

"No," the Prince replied. "My place is here with my people."

"You asked me to teach the Prince how to lead," Ackbar said to the Senator. "That is what I intend to do."

"I also asked you to keep him safe, Captain," the Senator added. "Remember that."

"All troops! Battle stations!" Kit Fisto ordered as he ignited his own lightsaber.

The Republic and Mon Calamari soldiers raised their weapons and lined up side by side, waiting for the order to attack. Prince Lee-Char grabbed a blaster and headed to the front line. He had to lead his people.

Captain Ackbar took his place alongside his Prince. "Do not fire until the Prince gives the command," he ordered the troops.

Ackbar watched as the Hydroid Medusas approached, waiting for the right moment. Prince Lee-Char stood nervously with the blaster. He'd never been in battle before.

Once the Hydroid Medusas were in range, Ackbar turned to the Prince. "Now, Your Highness."

Prince Lee-Char nodded at Captain Ackbar and yelled, "Attack!"

Following their Prince's command, the troops began firing on the Medusas. Blast after blast ricocheted of the creatures. Their weapons had no effect on the giant monsters.

Tamson, leading an army of aqua droids, came up behind the Hydroid Medusas. The Republic and Mon Calamari forces were outmatched.

Anakin and Ahsoka made their way back to the Prince. Their main objective was to ensure his safety.

"Ahsoka," Anakin called to his Padawan, "find a way out of here!"

Ahsoka moved in behind her Master, who was fending off an onslaught of Separatist blaster fire.

"Prince, where's somewhere safe?" Ahsoka asked.

"We can't retreat, not now!" Lee-Char demanded. "We've got to be brave!"

Ackbar hated to disobey his Prince, but he knew the Jedi were right. "There's a time to attack and a time to retreat," he said. "Now is not the time to be brave."

Lee-Char lowered his blaster. He knew that he could trust Captain Ackbar. "The safest place is in the caves," he said.

"I agree," Ackbar said. "Follow me."

Anakin and Kit Fisto continued to hold off the attack as the others followed Ackbar deeper down to the seafloor.

Kit looked to Anakin. "Go!" he said. "I'll hold them off." As a Nautolan, Kit Fisto was a superior underwater fighter.

Anakin didn't want to leave Master Fisto behind, but he knew the others needed his help.

"Come on!" Anakin called to the others as he swam past Ahsoka. "Keep going! Don't stop!"

CHAPTER SIX

The Mon Calamari town square was decimated by the time Nossor Ri and the Quarren forces arrived.

The aqua droids and Hydroid Medusas had driven the remaining Mon Calamari and clone troopers from the city center. What had once been a booming metropolis had been reduced to ruins.

Nossor Ri seemed pleased with the power of Tamson's Hydroid Medusas. Count Dooku had held up his end of the deal and delivered the Quarren a swift victory. From the looks of things, the battle was almost over.

Soon the Mon Calamari would surrender, and the bloodshed could end. It was unfortunate that it had to come to war, but the Mon Calamari would never have given up the throne otherwise.

He wondered if the Prince was still alive. He had no hard feelings toward the boy, and it was true that he and King Yos Kolina had been close friends. Perhaps he would even offer the boy a role in his new government, a way of reuniting the Quarren and Mon Calamari.

"Search the area for survivors," Nossor ordered his troops. "And secure the perimeter."

Riff Tamson swam up to the Quarren leader. "What took your squids so long?" Tamson asked, wondering why Nossor Ri and his troops stayed out of the battle. "You were told to assist in the invasion."

Nossor Ri was growing weary of Tamson. He was sent to the Quarren as an ambassador of the Separatists—an adviser. Now, he seemed to be asserting control over the whole military operation.

This was the Quarren's battle, and Nossor Ri was their leader. He was meant to command the military. If anything, Tamson and the droid army were meant to assist him.

"I didn't think you and your Separatist droids would need backup," Nossor Ri replied. "As it turns out, your reputation is a little exaggerated."

Tamson became angry. "Exaggeration is a

weapon of war," he said, baring his teeth. "It's what helped deliver the enemy into your hands."

"Then let's be thankful this is our day," Nossor replied. "A victorious day that—"

Suddenly Tamson grabbed Nossor Ri by the throat. "Disobey a command from Count Dooku again," he growled, "and I will kill you where you stand."

Nossor Ri struggled to breathe. Quarren guards quickly moved in to defend their leader. The Karkarodon just laughed. He released Nossor Ri, who stumbled back.

The Quarren leader took a few deep, labored breaths and watched Tamson swim off.

A sense of nausea spread through Nossor Ri. Perhaps he'd made an error in judgment allowing the Separatists to become involved in their struggle. Hopefully they would be leaving soon now that the battle was coming to an end.

Anakin led the others down to the coral caves that spread out like a vast system of mazes below Mon Calamari City.

"Even people who grew up around here would have a hard time finding their way around these caves," Captain Ackbar said. "We should be safe here for a while."

"Okay, everyone into that cave," Anakin ordered. "I'm going to wait here for Master Fisto and then we'll catch up to you."

As they filed into the cave, Anakin pulled Ahsoka aside. "Keep an eye on the Prince, will you?" he said. "I don't think Senator Tills is giving him the best guidance. Ackbar and the other Mon Calamari listen to what the Prince says, and we need to make sure what he's being told is the whole story."

"Understood, Master," she replied as she followed the others into the cave.

Anakin doubled back to see if he could find Kit Fisto. As he made his way back to the battle, the sounds of explosions rippling through the water became louder. At the center of the explosions, Anakin could make out a green light moving at amazing speeds.

Anakin knew right away that the green light was coming from Kit Fisto's lightsaber. He raced ahead to help out his fellow Jedi who was surrounded by at least a dozen aqua droids.

"I thought you could use some help," Anakin said as he cut through two of the droids.

"I thought I told you to go on ahead." Kit Fisto laughed. "I had everything under control."

Anakin used the Force to push one of the droids back at the others, causing them to explode. "It certainly looked that way."

"Well since you're here," Kit Fisto replied, "I guess I could use your help with these last few."

Together the two Jedi cut down the remaining aqua droids and then headed down toward the coral caves.

Deep in the underwater caves, the remaining Republic and Mon Calamari forces regrouped. Anakin, Kit Fisto, and Ahsoka worked to establish a base station. Clone troopers were posted at the cave entrance while Padmé, Senator Tills, and Ackbar sat with the Prince.

"We have to get word to the Council," Anakin said to the other Jedi. "We need to get a second round of reinforcements down here, and quick. Those creatures, whatever they were, are not Quarren. The Separatists are behind this, and if we don't move quickly, they will have a stranglehold over the whole system. This civil war could easily escalate into an interplanetary battle."

"I agree, the Council must be made aware of these recent developments," Kit Fisto said. He pulled out his comlink and tried to get a message off to the Jedi Council on Coruscant. "It would appear that the cave walls are blocking our communications. I might be able to get a better signal elsewhere in the cave."

"If we can't get a signal off, we're trapped," Padmé said. "How long can we stay here in this cave?"

"As long as the Prince's life is in jeopardy, I say we stay where we're safe," Senator Tills answered.

"With all due respect, Senator, we may have to fight our way out of here," Anakin added. "If we can't reach Master Yoda, then the only way to get to safety is to go through that army out there."

Senator Tills gave the Jedi a hard look.

"Master Jedi, you and the Republic were brought here to assist the Mon Calamari people," she said. "Now, I refuse to allow the Prince to be put in any further danger."

Captain Ackbar swam forward.

"The Senator is right. And so are the Jedi. We need to keep the Prince safe. That is our primary goal. He will lead the Mon Calamari to victory, of that I am sure. However, victory will not be achieved by sitting in a cave. If it comes down to it, we must be willing to fight—or even die for what we believe in. That is what King Kolina would have done and what I'm sure Prince Lee-Char will do as well."

The Prince rose and swam to the center of the cavern. "Everyone, please," he said. "I would like to give my thanks to the Jedi, to these brave soldiers, and all of you. I wish I could've done more for my people. Maybe then we would've been spared of all this—the illusion that I could actually lead in my father's place. I am not King Yos Kolina. I have failed you all and I have failed the people of Mon Cala."

"No," Ackbar said as he swam to the Prince's side. "Your father would be proud of you."

"Proud?" he asked. "But we lost!"

"Today you learned the hardest lesson a commander can learn," Ackbar replied. "How to live to fight another day. There will be more battles in this war, my young Prince. And we will be there to fight for you—all of us—because you are our leader."

"But how can we possibly win?" the Prince asked.

"I don't know," Ackbar said. "But I've seen your father come back from what seemed like crushing defeats more than once. I am confident that you'll figure out a way to win this war."

CHAPTER SEVEN

Riff Tamson sat on the King's throne in the Mon Calamari throne room as a hologram of Count Dooku was projected in front of him. A defeated-looking Nossor Ri stood at the Karkarodon's side.

The Quarren leader looked uneasy. Just hours earlier, he was the leader of a noble people fighting for their independence, and now he was unsure what he was.

Nossor Ri looked up to the throne and saw Riff Tamson sitting in that sacred chair. It was a chair where noble Kings had sat for generations.

It was true that Nossor Ri had wanted to do away with the Mon Calamari monarchy, but he hadn't wanted it to end like this. When his friend the King was murdered, he acted as though he had no idea who had committed the crime.

But it was perfect timing, wasn't it? he thought.

To Nossor Ri, Count Dooku's offer to aid the Quarren in their independence in exchange for joining the Separatist Alliance and the death of the King seemed to perfectly coincide. He knew that Dooku had been responsible for his friend's death. There was no other explanation.

Count Dooku stared out from the hologram at the two leaders of his invasion. The Separatist leader knew that Riff Tamson was strong and ruthless, but the Quarren seemed weak. Dooku could sense that the Quarren was second-guessing his choice to join them. Dooku needed to get this invasion over with quickly, then he could deal wih Nossor Ri.

"The young Prince, has he been captured?" Dooku asked his commander.

"No, my lord," Tamson replied. "Unfortunately, he escaped capture and is in hiding with what's left of the Jedi and their army."

Dooku's face hardened at the mention of the Jedi. He knew that Anakin Skywalker was among the survivors of the attack and that he would be the most difficult to stop.

"Do not underestimate this boy, Tamson,"

Dooku continued. "He must not become a symbol for the Mon Calamari people to rally behind."

"This child is but a coward. He is no leader," Tamson replied.

Dooku looked to the Karkarodon. "That is irrelevant. The whispering of his name can rekindle hope, and hope is something we cannot allow our enemy to possess."

Tamson nodded at the hologram of Dooku. "It will be taken care of, my lord. The planet will soon be ours. Once we round up the remaining Mon Calamari prisoners, there will be no place for him to hide and no people to rally behind him"

Nossor Ri could feel it all slipping away from him. Dooku and Riff Tamson were in control of Mon Cala now.

"Excuse me, Count Dooku, but what of the prisoners?" he asked.

"They are to be processed," Dooku replied. "Internment camps have been set up below the city. Gather all the prisoners there, then set them to work."

"Surely you do not mean all of them," Nossor Ri said. "The women and children—"

"They are to be sent as well," Dooku interrupted. "Is that understood?

Nossor Ri saw the fire burning in Dooku's eyes as he spoke. He began to worry that unless he played his cards right, he might not make it through this battle alive.

"Yes, my lord," Nossor replied.

Dooku could see that Nossor Ri understood the severity of his situation. He turned his stare to the Karkarodon.

"Tamson, I'm sending you reinforcements. Hold them in reserve and wait for the Republic's next move," Dooku added.

"As you wish, Count Dooku," Tamson replied as the hologram flickered off.

Ahsoka Tano, the Togruta Jedi, swam cautiously through the thick seaweed that grew out of the seafloor. Mon Cala was a long way from the Jedi Temple on Coruscant. She wondered if she would ever see sun-lit skies again. All she'd seen since they'd arrived on Mon Cala was dark, gray water.

This might be the longest that she'd ever stayed underwater, she thought. She didn't mind having to swim everywhere. Master Fisto and Captain Ackbar seemed to enjoy it, but Ahsoka looked forward to running and jumping on dry land again.

Movement in the distance pulled her back into the moment. She slowed down and sank deeper into the seaweed. Master Fisto had sent her out to survey the surrounding area. If they needed to make a quick escape, it would help to know the terrain.

As she got closer, she saw a school of small fish moving past. That was the only life she'd seen since leaving the cave. Once satisfied that she was alone, she turned around and headed back.

Ahsoka made her way through the maze of caves, passing the two scuba clones that stood guard on either side of the cavern that they'd converted into a command base.

As she entered, she smiled at Prince Lee-Char and came to a stop at his side. Jedi Master Kit Fisto stood off to the side and spoke to Mace Windu and Yoda via hologram. The signal was choppy, making it hard for the Jedi Master to report to the Council.

"We have lost contact with the clone troopers and Mon Calamari soldiers," Kit Fisto reported. "The Quarren ambushed us. They were ready to attack long before we were ever able to begin peace talks. Commander Monnk is among the missing as well."

The hologram flickered and briefly cut out.

"Desperate, the situation is," Yoda responded through the static. "Reinforce your position with clones unable—" The hologram crackled, and the audio cut out.

"Master, please repeat. Are you sending reinforcements?" Kit Fisto asked.

With that, the hologram faded. The cave walls were too thick to get a signal through. As long as they stayed hidden below, they would be cut off from the Jedi Council.

Prince Lee-Char approached the Jedi Master. Ahsoka and Captain Ackbar came up alongside him. The others hung back, listening.

"Are they coming?" the Prince asked. "Is the Republic sending more reinforcements?"

"I don't know," Kit Fisto replied.

"But they know our situation. They must know to send help," Lee-Char said.

Anakin stepped forward. He wanted to be hopeful and tell them that help was on the way, but he'd been in similar situations before. "Yeah . . . but it may take them a while to get here," he added. "We're gonna have to get ourselves to the surface and get off this rock."

Lee-Char turned to face Anakin. "I will not leave my people to die," he said. He looked to the others for support. He couldn't believe that the Jedi would be willing to abandon everyone on Mon Cala, including their own clone troopers.

"With all due respect, Your Highness," Anakin said, "if we stay, we all die. Once we get off this planet we can regroup, put together a proper invasion force, and return to rescue your people."

Padmé gave Lee-Char a reassuring look. "If we want to leave, first we need to get to the surface and see if our ship is still there," Padmé added. "That's our only hope."

"Okay, Padmé's right," Anakin said. "The first thing we need to do is get to that ship. I propose that we—"

Captain Ackbar interrupted. "The Prince will decide our course of action," he said.

Anakin and Padmé both looked at him. They'd hoped to have Ackbar's support for their plan.

Ackbar knew that the Jedi and Senator were right. The Prince would certainly be caught if they stayed on Mon Cala.

The captain moved closer to Lee-Char and added, "But we should probably take the Jedi's advice. There's not much that we can do for our people at this point."

The Prince stood silently and contemplated the situation. Eventually he looked to Padmé and Anakin. "I think it is best for us to try and escape using your ship," he said.

"As you wish, Your Highness," Anakin said. "Now follow me."

CHAPTER EIGHT

Far away from the battle on Mon Cala, the Jedi Council convened for an emergency meeting. They gathered at the Jedi Temple—a massive, spired structure that overlooked Coruscant, the capital of the Republic. For thousands of years the Temple had been home to the Jedi Order.

Made up of members from across the galaxy, the Jedi Order devoted their lives to mastering the Force. The Force was an energy field that surrounded all living things and bound the galaxy together. This energy is what gave the Jedi their power.

The Jedi began their training at a very young age. As children, they were taken from their homes and raised in the Jedi Temple. There they were taught how to control their emotions and how to become one with the Force.

Once they were old enough, the young Jedi became Padawan learners and were assigned to an older Jedi for training.

Eventually the Padawans would become Jedi Knights and maybe even Jedi Masters.

The most senior members of the Jedi Order were chosen to be on the Jedi Council. It was their responsibility to oversee all the Jedi throughout the galaxy.

Inside the Council chambers, Mace Windu sat next to Master Yoda while the remaining Jedi Masters—Obi-Wan Kenobi, Plo Koon, Adi Gallia, Luminara Unduli, and Saesee Tiin—flickered as holograms across the room.

The Council listened as Yoda explained the dire situation on Mon Cala. A hologram of the planet floated in front of him.

Not only were their fellow Jedi in danger, but the future of Mon Cala and the Mon Calamari people were also in jeopardy. The Jedi needed to find a solution to the conflict.

"We could try to assemble a second assault team, but our resources are stretched thin. As you all know, our clone troopers are committed to conflicts throughout the galaxy. It would take us days to outfit another clone regiment for underwater combat," Mace Windu said.

"Days our friends do not have," Obi-Wan Kenobi, Anakin's friend and former Master, added. "I fear that if we don't act quickly, we will have little chance of pulling off a successful rescue. Dooku surely will be expecting us, and the longer we wait, the more reinforcements he can amass."

"I agree with Master Kenobi," Plo Koon said.

Yoda nodded. The old Jedi meditated briefly on the problem. "Perhaps we should look to armies other than clones to help our cause," he said.

"What do you suggest?" Mace Windu asked.

Yoda gestured to the hologram of Mon Cala. The image quickly changed, and a map of the galaxy appeared in its place. Several blue planets spiraled, and then one glowing planet appeared red among the others.

"A suitable ally we must find to help with this mission," Yoda said.

Obi-Wan smiled slightly as he recognized the red planet on the hologram. It was a planet he knew well. "Naboo," he said.

"Yes," Yoda agreed. "To the Gungans, we must look."

"We shall contact them immediately," Mace Windu said.

Yoda held on to his cane with both hands and contemplated what was to come. Bringing more worlds into this conflict could cause greater problems than they could solve. There was already too much war in the galaxy.

Aqua droids and Quarren soldiers patrolled the maze of underwater caves looking for the Prince and the Jedi.

From the safety of the shadows, Padmé and Anakin watched as the Quarren and aqua droids passed. Anakin tried to plot the safest route from the caves, through the occupied city, and up to the surface.

"There are a lot of enemy troops between us and the surface," Padmé said.

"It's no problem," Anakin replied. "I just hope you're a fast swimmer."

Padmé smiled at Anakin. "Says the boy from the desert planet," Padmé added.

Padmé had met Anakin on the desert planet of Tatooine when they were both young children. She was with Obi-Wan Kenobi and his Master, Qui-Gon

Jinn, when they'd first found Anakin and discovered that he had Force ability. They had been close friends ever since.

Senator Tills swam up behind them. "Are you certain your ship is still there?" she asked.

"There's only one way to find out," Anakin said.

"I'll create a diversion so you can get past those patrols," Kit Fisto said, swimming up to meet them.

"All right," Anakin said to the Jedi Master. "Try to get a minisub or two. It'll help speed us to the surface."

"No problem," Kit Fisto replied as he swam off toward a patrol of Quarren soldiers.

As he got closer, Kit Fisto saw the Quarren were guiding along a group of captured clone troopers.

Through the cloudy water, he could make out Commander Monnk. Kit moved deftly through the water, remaining unseen as the patrol passed. He needed to find a way to free the prisoners.

Kit Fisto then moved into position beneath the oncoming Quarren guards. From there, he could see Commander Monnk coming along above him. He needed to get Monnk's attention without the Quarren spotting him. As the clone officer moved in closer, Kit Fisto positioned himself in the commander's sight and gave Monnk a little wave, letting the commander know to prepare for an escape.

Once he was ready, Kit Fisto tore out from his hiding spot and quickly dispatched a Quarren soldier riding a minisub. The other guards came at him.

Kit Fisto knocked them back and then used the Force to push the minisub downward through the water toward Anakin.

"Ahsoka, you're up first," Anakin ordered. "Take the Prince and Senator Tills."

Ahsoka hopped on the Quarren minisub as Lee-Char and Senator Tills grabbed onto the sides. Ahsoka hit the throttle and headed quickly for the surface.

Kit Fisto worked to release Commander Monnk before a second wave of Quarren reached them. Once the commander was free, Kit threw him a blaster.

"Commander, release your men and then follow me," Kit Fisto ordered the clone officer. "If we move quickly, we might just be able to hitch a ride off the planet. But first, I'll need to commandeer another one of those subs, so I'll need you to cover me."

"Understood, General," Commander Monnk

replied, quickly blasting the Quarren coming at him as he released his troops. The newly-freed scuba clones grabbed Quarren blasters and began fending off the Quarren guards.

"Okay, men, let's give the general some cover," the commander ordered the scuba clones.

"Roger that," the clones replied as they filled the water with blaster fire.

With his lightsaber ready, Kit Fisto headed toward the next group of Quarren soldiers with a minisub.

Blaster fire from the sub tore past him as he sliced through the Quarren soldiers in his way. The sub continued its assault as the Jedi swam straight for it. The Quarren pilot pulled on the throttle and tried to ram Kit.

As the minisub sped toward him, Kit Fisto maneuvered quickly past it and knocked the Quarren pilot from his seat. The sub spun out of control, but Kit Fisto used the Force to direct it toward Anakin.

Seeing the sub hurtling toward him, Anakin used the Force to pull it to them. He jumped into the pilot's seat and powered up the engine.

"Grab on," he called to Padmé and Captain Ackbar.

With Anakin at the controls, Padmé and Ackbar grabbed hold of either side of the sub and prepared for the climb to the surface.

Anakin pointed the sub toward the surface and sped off.

CHAPTER NINE

Inside the throne room, Tamson continued to plan the final leg of his invasion of Mon Calamari City. A hologram of the city and the coral base filled the center of the room.

Nossor Ri stood beside him, watching as the Karkarodon positioned his armies throughout Mon Cala.

"Are all these additional forces really necessary?" he asked Tamson. "Surely there are better uses for the Separatist armies elsewhere in the galaxy. The Mon Calamari Army and the Republic forces have been defeated. The Quarren Army can hold Mon Calamari City."

"Your Quarren soldiers are weak," Tamson replied. "That's why you accepted our offer of help in the first place. We will continue with our assault until all the Mon Calamari and Republic forces are either dead or captured."

"Doesn't that seem extreme? Wiping out half the population of a planet hardly seems right," Nossor Ri added. "All we wanted was a chance to rule Mon Cala . . . not whatever this invasion is."

A Quarren guard appeared from behind the hologram.

"Sir, the Jedi have reappeared with the Prince," he reported. "They are headed to the surface."

Tamson turned away from Nossor Ri. He had lost interest in the Quarren. "Bring them up on the scanner," he ordered.

The hologram changed to a diagram of the area outside the city. A pulsing red dot tracked the location of the Prince as he and the Jedi raced to the surface.

"Predictable." Tamson laughed. "Let them get within sight of their ship. I want them to watch their hope sink to the bottom of the sea."

The hologram changed again—this time revealing the Republic frigate hovering just above the surface.

The minisubs rose closer to the surface. As they passed the tops of the city buildings, they could make out the silhouette of the Republic frigate above them.

"There's the ship!" Padmé called out.

"It looks like it's still in one piece," Anakin replied.

Suddenly a blinding flash from above ripped through the frigate, exploding it into pieces. Large chunks of the ship crashed onto the surface of the water.

"Everyone, keep your heads down and hold on," Anakin called out as he pulled his sub away from the explosion.

He struggled to maneuver his minisub through the smoke-filled water. "Ahsoka, follow me," he called out to her.

"I'm right behind you, Master," she replied.

Anakin and Ahsoka tried to navigate their minisubs through the falling debris that rained down on them, but it was no use.

"The wreckage is coming down too hard," Anakin said. "I don't think we can get the subs through this mess."

"Agreed," Ahsoka replied. "I say we ditch them and swim for it."

"All right, everyone," Anakin said. "Let go of the

subs on my mark, and then we're going to swim for safety."

They released the subs and watched as they flew off and collided into the debris.

As they looked around, they could see aqua droids beginning to close in.

"Well, Prince, how do you feel about fighting again?" Anakin asked as he ignited his lightsaber and moved in to protect the group. Ahsoka ignited her own lightsaber and swam up next to her Master.

"Master Jedi," Lee-Char replied. "We're too vulnerable here. We must reach the seafloor."

Anakin looked around. "Okay, everyone, you heard the Prince," he called out. "We're heading back down to the seafloor. Grab onto the biggest piece of debris you can find and let it carry you to the bottom."

Anakin and Ahsoka deflected blasts from the aqua droids as the others grabbed hold of the large pieces of the exploded frigate that were falling to the seafloor.

"All right, Snips, your turn," Anakin said. "I'm right behind you."

"I'll race you to the bottom," Ahsoka said as she leaped onto the nearest piece of debris.

Blasts from the aqua droids ricocheted off the debris around him as he extinguished his lightsaber and grabbed hold of a falling piece of the ship. As the aqua droid blasts got closer, Anakin did his best to guide the debris toward the seafloor.

"I think I'm getting seasick!" he heard Padmé cry out as the current tossed them about.

"Just hold on," he called back. "It'll all be over before you know it."

Down on the seafloor, Kit Fisto, Commander Monnk, and several rescued scuba clones continued to fight off the Quarren guards. In the distance they noticed the debris falling toward them.

"Sir, what do you think that is?" Commander Monnk asked.

"I think it's the remains of our last chance to get off this planet," Kit Fisto replied. "We better go check it out."

"I suggest we hurry, sir," Monnk said, pointing to a team of aqua droids heading toward the crash site. "We're not the only ones interested in that debris."

They fought their way through the remaining Quarren patrol and swam out to examine the wreckage.

As they got closer, Kit Fisto spotted something moving on a piece of debris.

"Cover me, Commander," he said. "I'm going in to get a better look."

On his own, the Jedi was more easily able to navigate through the falling debris. Once inside the debris storm, he saw Prince Lee-Char clenching a piece of metal plating. He seemed to be unharmed. Behind the Prince he could make out Captain Ackbar and the two Senators—and finally Ahsoka follow by Anakin.

Kit Fisto swam up to the Jedi. Commander Monnk and the remaining scuba clones followed not far behind.

"Back so soon?" Kit Fisto joked to Anakin as he and Monnk grabbed hold of the debris.

"Yeah, the ship had some problems," Anakin replied.

"I can see that," Kit Fisto added. "All around me."

"The Separatists must have known we were coming," Ahsoka said. "But why didn't they wait until we were on the ship to blow it up?"

"They didn't want the Prince dead," Kit Fisto replied. "At least not dead like that. Dooku wants to make an example of him. Execute him in front of his own people."

"There's a squad of droids heading our way," Commander Monnk reported. "They should be on us right after we hit the bottom."

Captain Ackbar pushed off the debris that he was holding and swam to the Jedi. "Our only hope is to split up," he said. "The droids will be searching for us, and it's best if we give them multiple targets. We must get the Prince into hiding."

"I'm not sure that's the best strategy," Anakin replied.

"I am sure," the Prince spoke up. "Captain Ackbar's words are my own. It will give us the best chance of surviving if we split up."

"As you wish." Anakin nodded to the Prince and then called to his Padawan. "Ahsoka, you and the Prince go with Master Fisto and take the clones with you. I'll take the Senators and Captain Ackbar. Lay low. Our only hope is that Master Yoda can send help in time."

"No," Captain Ackbar corrected him. "Prince Lee-Char is our only hope."

Ahsoka, the Prince, Kit Fisto, and Monnk let go of the debris first. The rest followed shortly after.

The debris impacted the ground hard, causing the water to be thick with silt and difficult to see through.

The aqua droids quickly closed in on the site of the impact. As the water cleared, there wasn't a trace of the Prince or any of the Jedi.

CHAPTER TEN

Inside the glass, bubble-shaped High Tower Boardroom in the underwater Gungan capital of Naboo, a hologram of Yoda stood front and center before the Gungan High Council.

The Republic world of Naboo was located not far from Mon Cala in the Outer Rim of the galaxy. It was home to many races, including the Gungans, who were an amphibian race that lived in the planet's deep lakes.

The Gungan capital, or Otoh Gunga as it was known, was the largest of the underwater cities on Naboo. It was built deep in Lake Paonga on the edge of Naboo's Lianorm Swamp. The city was constructed out of a system of glowing, bubble-shaped buildings that were anchored to massive stone pillars attached to the lake's floor.

The Gungans were a secluded people and disliked getting involved in the business of others. A failed Separatist invasion of Naboo years earlier had forced them to embrace the Republic and the outside world, but they still remained weary of becoming too involved in the Clone Wars.

The head of the Gungan High Council and leader of the Gungan people was Boss Lyonie. In the Boardroom, he sat at the center of a raised platform that overlooked the rest of the chamber. Surrounding him were the other members of the Council, all dressed in ceremonial robes. By the Boss's side sat Jar Jar Binks.

Jar Jar was the Gungan representative to the Republic and was close friends with both Padmé, the Republic Senator from Naboo, and Anakin.

They had met years earlier during the attempted Separatist invasion of Naboo and had remained friends ever since.

Unlike other Gungans, Jar Jar enjoyed adventure and space exploration, and he often traveled on diplomatic missions with Senator Amidala and Anakin.

Boss Lyonie leaned his head forward and addressed the hologram of the Jedi Master.

"Master Yoda, sir," the Boss said to the hologram. "To what's we owin' the pleasure of your transmission?"

"Your help, the Republic needs," Yoda replied.

Jar Jar's eyes lit up. He wondered what kind of mission the Republic was going to send him on. Since becoming a Republic representative, he'd traveled across the galaxy with Padmé and Anakin.

Boss Lyonie seemed less enthusiastic.

"Something's a-tell meesa big help you need, no?" he asked.

"Senator Amidala, your longtime ally, trapped on an occupied planet she is," Yoda revealed. "Reinforcements from the Grand Gungan Army the Republic needs. Dire the situation is."

Jar Jar jumped up. He was ready to go rescue Padmé. "Meesa—" he began, but the Boss raised his hand and quieted the representative.

"Mmmm . . ." Lyonie contemplated the Jedi's request. "Weesa needs some thinking time to respond to deesa news." The Boss looked to the other members of the Council who nodded in agreement. It wasn't that they didn't want to help Senator Amidala—Padmé had long been a friend and supporter of the Gungan people in the Galactic

Senate—but the Gungans did not like to fight the battles of others.

Jar Jar couldn't believe what he was hearing. He turned to the Boss. "Thinking? Nosa thinking!" he said. "Meesa thinking Padmé would help us! Has helped us! Big time! Weesa gots to help her now!"

Boss Lyonie thought about what Jar Jar had said. He leaped to his feet. He was deadly serious. "Yousa right," he said. "Thinking timesa done! Weesa need to be leavin' now!"

Yoda gave the members of the Gungan Council a pleased look. The Grand Gungan Army was their last hope.

Back on Mon Cala, Kit Fisto led Ahsoka, Prince Lee-Char, Commander Monnk, and two scuba clones back down into the underwater caves below the city. As they passed through the entranceway, the Nautolan Jedi paused and surveyed the water outside.

"I don't think we've been followed," Kit Fisto said. "Commander Monnk, post a lookout."

The Commander ordered one of the clone troopers to guard the entrance to the cave and sent a second to stand lookout at the rear entrance.

Ahsoka led the Prince deeper into the safety of the coral cavern. Kit Fisto followed not far behind.

"Ahsoka, your main responsibility is protecting the Prince," the Jedi said. "Keep him in your sight at all times. This cave should provide safety for the foreseeable future, but we can never be too cautious."

"Yes, Master," Ahsoka replied.

"What are we going to do now?" the Prince asked. "We have no army, and we don't know if reinforcements are coming. What are our options?"

"We sit tight," Ahsoka replied. "There's not much we can do."

Prince Lee-Char was exasperated. He didn't want to sit and wait. His people were in danger, and he needed to find a way to save them. "How can we just sit here? Either we have to find another way to get off the planet and get help, or we have to try and save the Mon Calamari ourselves. Isn't that what Master Anakin said earlier?"

"I'm sure Anakin is working on a plan to get us out of here," Ahsoka replied. "That's what he does best."

"In the meantime," Kit Fisto added, "you need to stay in the safety of the cave."

From the cave entrance, Commander Monnk saw a group of aqua droids coming closer.

Monnk and the clone trooper guard hid among the seaweed. Trying not to be spotted, they stayed low. The clones watched as the droids passed and then followed at a safe distance. Commander Monnk wanted to see where these droids were headed.

The clones moved in behind the droids and saw them with what looked like a group of prisoners.

Commander Monnk cautiously made his way back to the cave. "Sir, you better come see this," he said.

"Stay here and keep an eye on the Prince," Kit Fisto said to Ahsoka.

"Wait," the Prince replied. "I'm not staying here. I can't live my life in hiding."

"Sir, this is something the Prince should probably see," Commander Monnk added.

Kit Fisto, Ahsoka, and Lee-Char followed Monnk out of the cave entrance.

Hiding out of sight, they laid low against the coral floor. There they saw aqua droids and Quarren soldiers guiding captured Mon Calamari and clones. They were being herded like cattle into the depths beyond the edge of the city.

"There are so many prisoners," Lee-Char said. "Where are they taking them?"

"To become slaves," Kit Fisto replied. "They will most likely be sent to work in the ore mines."

"What? There are children over there," Lee-Char said. "I can't believe Nossor Ri and the Quarren agreed to this!"

"Count Dooku rules here now," Ahsoka added. "Not the Quarren."

Kit Fisto's usual smile fell. "What you see, Prince," he said, "is the future of all the people on this world, Mon Calamari and Quarren. They will all become slaves for Count Dooku."

The Prince just watched as the prisoners were moved out.

"Come on," Kit Fisto added. "Let's get back before we're spotted."

Inside the caves, Prince Lee-Char spoke quietly with Ahsoka while Commander Monnk and Kit Fisto watched the enemy from the cave's mouth.

"All those people being turned into slaves," the Prince said to Ahsoka. "There must be something more I can do. I refuse to just sit here."

"I know it's hard, but you have to be patient," she replied.

"But you saw my people," Lee-Char said. "I've failed them.

"No," Ahsoka said. "Remember Captain Ackbar's words. You are the last hope of your people. As long as you live they will endure."

"I need an army," the Prince said. "We have to fight back."

"You don't have to carry a sword to be powerful," the young Jedi said. "Some leaders find strength in inspiring greatness in others."

"But my people don't even know I'm alive," he said. "How can I inspire them if they think I am dead?"

CHAPTER ELEVEN

The vast coral seafloor spread out below Mon Calamari City. The Lower City, as it was known, was a dark, shadowy place that offered protection from the squads of aqua droids that patrolled in search of survivors.

Through the shadows, Anakin led Captain Ackbar, Padmé, and Senator Meena Tills through the barren and rubble-filled Lower City. The Jedi appeared to be searching for something.

"I don't understand what we're doing down here," Padmé said as they swam through the debris. "We need to find a way to contact the Jedi Council or at least find a ship that can get us off this planet."

"And we must protect the Prince," Senator Tills reminded them. "His safety is of paramount importance. Do you think your fellow Jedi will be able to protect him, Master Skywalker? Captain Ackbar or I should have stayed with him. I don't know why you split us up like that."

"The Prince is in good hands, Senator," Anakin replied. "Master Fisto and my Padawan, Ahsoka, will make sure he remains safe."

"They better," Senator Tills said. "Otherwise there is no hope for the Mon Calamari people."

"So what are we doing down here?" Padmé asked for a second time. "It doesn't seem like there's much down here—except for some abandoned buildings."

"Trust me," Anakin replied. "I have a plan."

"Your plans usually end in you blowing something up," Padmé added.

Anakin smiled as he surveyed the underwater cityscape. "Captain Ackbar," he said. "Which of these structures houses the city's interplanetary scanners?"

"It's over there, across the square," Ackbar replied. "Why?"

"Well," Anakin explained, "just in case Master Yoda is sending reinforcements, I thought it would be helpful if the enemy couldn't tell they were coming."

Ackbar nodded in agreement. "If we knock out that radar, they won't see our reinforcements until they're right on top of the city."

"That's assuming someone is coming," Senator Tills added.

"I'm sure Master Yoda will find a way to send help," Padmé reassured the group, although she secretly worried that their last transmission hadn't made it to the Jedi Council. The Separatist's hold on Mon Cala continued to grow. Even a full-on invasion of the planet might not be enough to stop them. Anakin and the other Jedi are their only hope for survival, she thought. There is nothing more the Prince or the Mon Calamari people can do.

Anakin led the group around some of the buildings to get a clearer look at the base of the tower that Captain Ackbar had pointed out.

As they got close, they could see where the building connected to the reef. The giant structure was attached to the planet itself.

"Okay, cover me," Anakin said as he stood facing the base of the tower. "I'm going to have to concentrate."

"Concentrate?" Padmé asked. "Concentrate on what?"

"On bringing that building down," Anakin replied.

Padmé rolled her eyes. "Of course you're going to knock down a building," she said. "That's not going to draw any attention to us."

Captain Ackbar moved the others out of the way as Anakin raised his arms toward the building.

The Jedi closed his eyes and concentrated. In his mind, he could see the tower breaking loose from the coral that held it in place.

Around him, the water started to ebb and flow under the pressure of the Force. Suddenly one of the building's support beams wrenched. The bending metal let out a large groan that echoed through the water.

Picking up on the disturbance, a team of aqua droids moved in to investigate.

"We have company," Captain Ackbar said as he spotted the approaching droids.

Anakin strained under the mass of the building. He needed to bring it down before the aqua droids realized what was happening.

"Anakin, hurry!" Padmé called out as the droids spotted the Jedi and began firing at him.

Anakin couldn't stop. He could feel the building

coming free of its supports. All he needed was a little more time.

Captain Ackbar and Padmé moved in to cover him with blaster fire.

Anakin focused all his energy on the building. Instantly everything seemed calm.

He twisted his hand, and the massive metal support crumbled. Twisting and groaning, the structure cracked and broke free of the coral reef. Finally it fell, collapsing into a neighboring building.

In the throne room, Tamson and Nossor Ri stood in front of the hologram of the area surrounding Mon Calamari City.

Nossor Ri paced back and forth as Tamson scrutinized the position of all his troops on the battlefield.

"Without their ship, I doubt the Jedi will be able to get the Prince off this planet," Tamson said. "We made sure of that. There are only so many places that he can hide. My aqua droids will find him eventually."

"And then what?" Nossor Ri asked him.

"Then the planet and its ore mines are under our control," Tamson replied.

"Is that all this is about for you?" the Quarren added. "Our ore mines?"

The Karkarodon laughed. "You're a fool, Nossor," he said, "if you ever thought it was about anything else. No one cares about your stupid world."

Suddenly all the lights in the throne room blinked on and off before going dead. The hologram fizzled and faded. A moment later, the emergency lighting came up.

Tamson was enraged. "What's happening?!" he barked to an aqua droid who monitored their command base's systems. "Report!"

The droid pressed several buttons on the command console, which remained unresponsive. "We have lost all radar and sonar scanning, sir," it replied.

His frustration growing, Tamson lunged toward the droid with his teeth bared. It appeared that he might bite it in two. "Reestablish the connections," he ordered.

"We cannot, sir," the droid answered as it tried to get some response from the console.

"Why not?" Tamson asked as he anxiously circled the room.

"The building that housed the radar is gone," the droid answered, seemingly surprised by what he saw on the display screen.

"How could a building be gone?" Nossor Ri asked. "The Mon Calamari military doesn't have the resources left to blow up a building."

"Apparently they do," the Karkarodon snapped back as he spun to face Nossor Ri and the rest of the Quarren in the room.

"There's no reason to think that this was the Mon Calamari's doing," Nossor Ri added. "I'm sure it's just a problem with the sensor relays. The city's taken a lot of damage today, there's bound to be problems with some of its systems."

"As I said, you're a fool. Without our sensors, we're blind," he barked. "We need to prepare for an attack!"

"Let's just send a team out to investigate," Nossor Ri said. "There was nothing on the scope prior to the attack."

"That's precisely why we must assume an attack is imminent!" Tamson said. "Guards to me!"

Four Quarren guards moved to Tamson's side as he pushed past Nossor Ri and headed toward the exit.

"Where are you going?" Nossor Ri asked.

"To find that meddling Prince and his Jedi friends," Tamson replied. "I need you to stay here and get these scanners up and running again. Contact me the second you have them working."

Tamson swam out of the room with the Quarren guards in tow.

CHAPTER TWELVE

Prince Lee-Char stood alone at the mouth of the cave. In his hand, he held a large conch shell.

In days gone by, that was how his people would signal to one another. The sound of the shell was symbolic—a way of reminding the Mon Calamari who they were. He'd seen his father blow conch shells at many ceremonial gatherings.

To many, the sound of the conch shell meant the arrival of the King.

As much as he tried, Lee-Char did not feel like a King. He felt more like a boy wearing his father's uniform.

The Prince looked down at the conch shell in his hand and then off to the distance where he could see the Mon Calamari prisoners and the Quarren guards.

If he was truly going to take his father's place and lead the Mon Calamari, he needed to make his stand. He needed to finally step out from the shadows and let his people know that he was ready to lead them to freedom.

He slowly raised the conch shell to his mouth and blew into it as hard as he could. The sound of the shell echoed through the murky water. Out in the open water, the Mon Calamari prisoners stopped as they and the guards turned to look over to where the sound was coming from. They all knew what the sound of the conch meant. The shell sounded again, and one of the prisoners spotted the Prince.

"It's the Prince!" the prisoner cheered. "Look everyone! The Prince has come to rescue us!"

From deeper in the cave, Ahsoka, too, heard the conch blast.

"Oh no!" she called to the others. "The Prince! Hurry!"

Kit Fisto, Ahsoka, and Commander Monnk hurried to the mouth of the cave. As they arrived, they could see Lee-Char addressing the prisoners.

The Quarren guards looked on in surprise. They didn't expect to see the Prince standing unprotected just a short distance from the prison camp.

"People of Mon Cala!" he began. "All people of Mon Cala who would not be slaves, have hope! You will not be prisoners much longer! You must have faith that we can overcome this tyranny. None of us have to be slaves to the Separatists. Not Mon Calamari and not the Quarren. I give you my word that I will free you all."

The prisoners began to cheer.

"Okay, I think the show is over," Ahsoka said as she grabbed the Prince by the shoulders and pulled him back into the cave. "The guards will be coming. We have to go."

Kit Fisto and Commander Monnk moved into a defensive position around the Prince as the Quarren guards and aqua droids headed toward the cave's entrance. The Jedi and clones were gravely outnumbered.

"Ahsoka, get the Prince into the caves and keep moving," Kit Fisto said. "We'll hold off the Quarren as long as we can."

Ahsoka wanted to stay and fight. They were definitely outnumbered, but she thought that they might stand a chance if she were there.

Kit Fisto sensed her hesitation. "You have to go, Padawan," he said. "You have to go now."

"Be safe, Master," she said as she turned to head deeper into the cave. Out of the corner of her eye, she spotted something in the water. It looked like hundreds of tiny dots moving toward them.

"Sir, there's something coming this way," one of the scuba clones said. "And there's a lot of them."

A smile grew on Kit Fisto's face as the mysterious army approached. "Gungans!" he called to the others. "It seems that the tide has turned in our favor!"

The Quarren guards and aqua droids retreated back toward the prison camp as the Gungans swam in around them.

"We need to move quickly while we have the upper hand," Kit Fisto added. "Let's get those prisoners free. The more soldiers we have, the better we'll be."

"You heard the general," Commander Monnk called to the scuba clones. "Let's go free our brothers in arms."

The clones raised their weapons and charged at the prison gates.

Kit Fisto turned to the Prince. "You wanted to free your people," he said. "Well, here's your chance."

"Free my people!" The Prince cheered as he swam out of the cave and followed behind the clones. Ahsoka swam after him, her two lightsaber blades glowing in the water.

Kit Fisto charged for the front lines. Around him, the Gungan Army quickly overwhelmed the Quarren and aqua droids. The Gungans were some of the best underwater warriors in the galaxy.

He approached the Gungan commander who barked orders to his men.

"Your timing couldn't have been better," he said. "It's an honor to fight alongside the Grand Gungan Army."

"The honor isa ours, Master Jedi," the general said. "Where'sa the Senator? Weesa needen to rescue her."

"That's a very good question," the Jedi replied.

Aqua droids closed in around the destroyed scanner building. Igniting his lightsaber, Anakin positioned himself next to Captain Ackbar in front of the others.

Padmé and Senator Tills headed for the safety of the rubble. In the distance, several Hydroid Medusas approached.

"At least we're taking attention away from the Prince," Padmé joked.

Anakin, Padmé, Senator Tills, and Captain Ackbar watched helplessly as the Hydroid Medusas closed in around them. They knew that they had no defense against these giant creatures.

Suddenly, an explosion got their attention. Something was blowing up the Hydroid Medusas.

Anakin scanned the water until he saw a familiar face heading their way.

"I guess Master Yoda got our message after all," he said. Then, turning to Padmé, he added, "Now aren't you glad I blew up that building?"

A team of Gungan warriors descended on them. They threw large blue balls of plasma energy called Boomas at the Hydroid Medusas. These balls exploded into various shapes, colors, and sizes as they lit up the underwater landscape.

Through the explosions, Jar Jar spotted Anakin. "Ani!" he called to his old friend. "Meesa so happy to see you!"

"Perfect timing, Jar Jar," Anakin said.

"Whassa?" Jar Jar asked, shaking his head. "Meesa can't hear so good since we submergify."

In the throne room, Nossor Ri worked to reestablish some of the holo scanners. There was no turning back, he thought. The Separatists were a fact of life now. Even after they'd rebuilt the world, their armies would be on Mon Cala—at least until they'd mined the planet dry.

Accessing the Mon Calamari backup scanner system, Nossor Ri activated a static-ridden hologram of the battle that filled the room.

Immediately, red blips appeared across the map. They surrounded the Separatist forces. One by one, the Hydroid Medusas blinked and vanished from the hologram.

Nossor Ri activated his comlink. "Tamson, Tamson, come in!" he said. "Where are you? The Republic reinforcements are overwhelming our defenses! We must retreat! We must retreat now!"

A shaky holographic image of Riff Tamson appeared in front of him. "I warned you this attack was coming," he said. "Where are the Jedi concentrating their attack?"

Nossor Ri studied the scanner. "There are two groups of Jedi," an aqua droid reported. "One in the lower city center and the other is releasing the prisoners near the coral base."

"The prisoners?" Tamson said. "The Prince must be with them. I'm committing the reinforcements that Count Dooku sent to the attack. He will not be able to escape this time."

CHAPTER THIRTEEN

The battle raged on around the city. The Grand Gungan Army and liberated prisoners worked together to take care of the remaining Hydroid Medusas.

The cheers from the Gungan warriors filled the water as the lifeless bodies of the giant creatures tumbled to the seafloor.

Ahsoka and Prince Lee-Char moved through the smoke-filled water.

As they swam off, two Quarren soldiers on a minisub locked their sights on the Prince. Blaster fire tore past Lee-Char's head as Ahsoka pulled him out of the way.

Seeing the attack on the Prince, Kit Fisto charged at the sub. The Nautolan tore through the water and blocked the blasts with his lightsaber. The sub kept firing blast after blast, but the Jedi continued to stay ahead of it, blocking all its attacks.

Seeing that the Prince had vanished into the dark water, the sub pilot turned and headed back toward the main battle, but Kit Fisto was on top of them before they could get too far. With one slice of his lightsaber, the sub exploded.

Ahsoka and Lee-Char watched as the sub exploded in the distance. The Prince stopped swimming and turned to the Jedi. "There's no point in running, Ahsoka," he said. "The battle always comes to us." He turned around, grabbed a blaster from the debris, and charged into battle.

Ahsoka ignited her two lightsabers and followed after the Prince.

"I hope you know what you're doing," she said.

They made their way to Kit Fisto, who led the charge of Gungans and prisoners against the Quarren and Separatist forces. The Nautolan Jedi's lightsaber lit up the water as it tore through the oncoming aqua droids.

Suddenly, a large shadow moved in above them. Ahsoka looked up and saw a giant Trident drill ship descending toward them. The squidlike ship began to turn slowly as its tentacle legs spread wide, revealing its Trident drill. The ship picked up speed and began to spin like a massive propeller. The water swelled, catching Ahsoka, Kit Fisto, and Prince Lee-Char in its wake.

"Stay in the center!" Ahsoka called out. "There's less turbulence!"

She reached for the Prince but the current was too powerful for her to move. Realizing that he was out of reach, she began to concentrate. Trying to block out everything around her, she forced all her energy on the Prince.

Using the power of the Force, Ahsoka began to push the Prince to the center of the now almost completely formed funnel. Lee-Char looked up to see the bottom of the Trident drill open.

Riff Tamson came flying out of the bottom of the drill and headed straight for the Prince. He grabbed the Prince by the shoulders as they collided.

Lee-Char wriggled his way free, and Tamson swooped around for another pass using the thick, dark water as cover.

Ahsoka spotted the Karkarodon preparing for another attack on the Prince. She cut through a group of aqua droids and used the Force to push Tamson away from the Prince.

"Nice try, Jedi," Tamson said. "But I grow tired of playing games with you and the Prince." He pressed a button on his comlink, commanding all of the surrounding aqua droids to turn on Ahsoka and the Prince.

Tamson vanished again into the dark water. While Ahsoka fended off the droid fire, Tamson came out of the dark water and cornered the Prince.

As the Karkarodon's jaws snapped, Kit Fisto tore through the dark and hit Tamson in the side. While Tamson recovered from the first hit, Kit Fisto swam past again, landing a fist on Tamson's jaw.

Filled with fury, Tamson chased after Kit Fisto, leaving the Prince behind.

As Tamson pursued Kit Fisto, Ahsoka doubled back toward the Prince. A team of aqua droids appeared from the dark water and blocked her path. From the corner of his eye, Tamson noticed that Lee-Char was unguarded. He knocked past Kit Fisto in a desperate attempt to get to the Prince.

Kit Fisto caught Tamson's foot, spun himself around, and knocked the Karkarodon away from the Prince.

"Ahsoka, escape with the Prince!" Kit Fisto called out. "I'll hold him off."

Without hesitation, Ahsoka shot an ascension cable to the seafloor.

She grabbed the Prince and used the cable's retraction to pull them down.

Kit Fisto watched Ahsoka and the Prince vanish into the darkness as a squad of aqua droids surrounded him. He ignited his lightsaber and strategically moved toward the approaching droids. He sliced through the first few but quickly noticed more and more descending upon him. Soon there were too many for him to fight off. He tried to navigate through them, hoping to escape back into the dark, cloudy water. It was too late. The droids had him. He was now their prisoner.

"Wassa 'dat?" Jar Jar called as he saw a Trident drill ship moving in above them. "Meesa no liken look-a dat big monsta ship."

Anakin and Captain Ackbar turned to see the ship right as it began to spin. Eventually the water around them swirled into a cone.

"This isn't good," Anakin said. "If we don't get out of here that thing will rip us to bits."

"It would seem that our advantage didn't last for very long," Captain Ackbar added.

Behind them, the Separatist Army regrouped. Anakin and Ackbar fought through the water as the Gungan soldiers were spun about and smashed into buildings. Coming toward them, they saw Jar Jar pushing through the spiraling water.

Padmé struggled against the current, and the Trident drill ship whirled above her. The watery cone pulled and spun around her, knocking her from side to side. "Anakin!" she called as the current swept her off.

Anakin struggled to reach her. He used all his power to propel himself against the current, but she vanished into the dark water before he could break free of the raging water. "Padmé!" he yelled as she vanished from his sight.

"Meesa go find her," Jar Jar called as he swam off into the darkness.

Ackbar swam back against the current and called to Anakin. "We've got one chance to stop this ship," he said. "Follow my lead."

Anakin took Ackbar's lead and followed the Mon Calamari toward the churning drill.

As the current got stronger, Anakin held on to Ackbar's back as they fought against it and struggled to swim up toward the Trident ship.

When they got close, Ackbar called out, "Sever one of the legs!"

Anakin launched from Ackbar's back toward the bottom of the drill. He made his way up a bit before letting go.

The current spun him out, and he swung his lightsaber at one of the legs as he passed by. The leg exploded, causing a chain reaction that destroyed the drill and making the ship fly wildly out of control toward the ocean floor.

The Trident drill ship smashed against the coral that rose from the seafloor. Thick, black smoke mixed with the water.

"Padmé," Anakin called through the darkness. She couldn't have gone too far, he thought.

As the smoke cleared, Anakin could see two figures swimming toward him.

"Anakin," a voice called out. It was Padmé. She and Jar Jar floated in the water in front of him. "Watch out," she said. "It's a trap."

Anakin spun around, his lightsaber lighting the water around them.

Through the murky water he could make out the shapes of multiple aqua droids moving in from all directions.

He slashed at the first few that moved in, but it was too late. They had already captured Jar Jar and Padmé.

The droids were on him as the water cleared. In the distance he could see Captain Ackbar fending off another squad of aqua droids. He hoped his friend would fare better than he had.

CHAPTER FOURTEEN

Outside the city, aqua droids and Quarren guards assembled the captured Mon Calamari, Gungan, and clone prisoners. Then they were to be led off to prison camps that had been set up around the outskirts of the city.

Tamson swam up alongside a line of prisoners being escorted by aqua droids. Behind him, he pulled a captured Kit Fisto.

The Karkarodon was pleased with his capture. He tugged on his prisoner's restraints, but the Jedi stood calmly and refused to struggle. Tamson pulled the Jedi closer, but Kit Fisto just smiled and remained unflinching. This only served to aggravate Tamson, who enjoyed watching his enemy suffer at his hands.

"Enjoy yourself while you can, Jedi," Tamson said as he leaned in close to Kit Fisto and bared his razor-sharp teeth. "I have a special prison waiting for you. Soon you will experience suffering beyond anything you could imagine."

He handed the Jedi off to an aqua droid who put him in with the other prisoners.

"Make sure you put him with the other Jedi and the Senator. I have big plans for them." Tamson turned to another team of droids. "And, you, go find the Prince!" he yelled.

Ahsoka and Lee-Char hid in the darkness of a cave and watched as Kit Fisto was escorted off by the aqua droids.

"Now you and I are the only ones left," the Prince said.

"I'm sorry, Lee-Char," she replied. "I know that you want to save your people, but right now I need to find a way to save you. That is my mission. I promised my Master that I'd keep you safe."

"But I know what I must do," the Prince said. "I must lead. My people need me. It's just that I don't know how to win this war."

"Look," Ahsoka said. "I know you're scared, but you can't let your fear control you."

"Aren't you scared?" Lee-Char asked her.

"I used to be. All the time," she replied. "Until I realized that if you make decisions out of fear, you're more likely to be wrong."

Lee-Char thought about that for a moment. "I will unify Mon Cala again, I promise."

There were too many aqua droids searching for the Prince. Ahsoka had to get him to safety.

"We have to go," Ahsoka said, leading him deeper into the safety of the cave.

Lee-Char turned to take one more look at his captured army.

Ahsoka and Lee-Char swam through the coral caves and found safety under a platform in the city's main thoroughfare. Hidden in the shadows, they watched as a platoon of aqua droids swam by. Miraculously, they remained unnoticed.

"We can't hide forever," Prince Lee-Char said.

"The Gungan Army was the last of the Republic's reinforcements. There won't be any more," Ahsoka said. "The battle is over—and I'm sorry to say that we lost. I can't rescue everyone on my own and protect you at the same time. Our only hope is that we can contact Master Yoda. Now we have to find a way to get off this planet."

"The failure is mine," Lee-Char said. "It's not the Republic's or anyone else's fault. I was meant to lead this world as my father had. It was my responsibility and I failed."

Ahsoka noticed more prisoners being escorted by. "Get back," she said.

They hid again as a group of clones, Gungans, and Mon Calamari were led past and down into the lower depths. Once they'd passed, Lee-Char and Ahsoka swam to a new hiding place under a tube connector.

Once in the safety of the tube connector, Lee-Char said, "If my father were here, he could unite with Nossor Ri and the Quarren. The Quarren and Mon Calamari have always had a difficult relationship, but it was respectful. That was until Riff Tamson arrived. Once that Karkarodon got inside Nossor Ri's head, the alliance between the Mon Calamari and Quarren fell apart."

"The Quarren are being used," Ahsoka told him. "Dooku will betray them as well. I've seen it happen before."

Lee-Char thought for a moment. "If we're going to make it through this, I must reunite the Mon Calamari and Quarren people."

Ahsoka was unsure. Anakin had told her to keep the Prince safe and that meant keeping him away from the battle. But she knew Lee-Char had a point, if they could unite the Mon Calamari and the Quarren, then they might have a chance at taking down the Separatists.

"Okay, I like your thinking," Ahsoka said, deciding to go along with the Prince. "But what's the strategy?"

"Count all the prisoners," he said. "Mon Calamari, Gungans, and clones. If we all fought together, we would outnumber our opponent."

"If this is going to work," Ahsoka replied, "we'll need to let your people know. They'll need to be ready to fight."

"We need Captain Ackbar," Lee-Char said. "And I think I know where to find him."

Kit Fisto, Anakin, Padmé, and Jar Jar were among columns of prisoners that were led into the Mon Calamari Senate chambers. Once inside, they were separated from the other Mon Calamari, Gungan, and clone prisoners. A group of aqua droids escorted them into a makeshift prison in the center of the chamber.

Riff Tamson was waiting for them when they arrived. "Bring them to me," he ordered the droids.

The aqua droids used their heavy grips to muscle the prisoners over to Tamson and Nossor Ri.

"A Senator, two Jedi Knights, and a fumbling amphibian. I would have thought the Prince would be easier to capture than the four of you." Tamson laughed.

Anakin looked the Separatist leader square in the eyes. He wasn't intimidated by the hulking Karkarodon. "It must be part of our plan," he replied.

"I had the exact same thought . . . ," Tamson said as he shoved Padmé and Jar Jar toward two Quarren soldiers.

"Let go of her!" Anakin yelled as he broke from the droid's grasp. He charged toward Padmé, but two Quarren guards crossed their weapons, blocking his path. The aqua droids were on him before he could do anything more. Tamson smiled. He could sense Anakin's feelings for Padmé.

"Rack 'em up," he said.

The Quarren Guards pushed Padmé and Jar Jar into two mechno crab traps. These prisons resembled giant, mechanical, almost droidlike crabs that could hold prisoners in place. Jar Jar and Padmé were each forced to stand on pedestals that resembled the tip of a Trident drill. Above them floated what looked like the top half of the crab. Two mechanical arms hung down from each. At the end, giant claws pinched around their arms, suspending them above the bottom half. The prisoner's feet barely touched the pedestal. From the top of each trap, two mechanical eyestalks protruded out. At the end, two yellow, droidlike eyes kept watch over the prisoners.

"Let me go!" Padmé yelled to the guards as the trap's claws closed around her arm, but her pleas went unheard.

"Meesa don't like this," Jar Jar said. "Oh deesa pinchy grabby."

Anakin struggled against his restraints. "Tamson! Leave them alone!"

"Do not worry, Jedi," Tamson replied. "There's plenty of suffering to go around."

As Tamson spoke, two cages constructed out of what appeared to be electric eels rose up from the lower levels of the room. The two Jedi were guided toward the cages. As they got close, Anakin and Kit Fisto could see the eels crackle with electricity.

One of the eels snapped at Anakin as he was pushed closer. The Quarren guards forced the Jedi inside.

"Now tell me." Tamson smiled at his prisoner's discomfort. "Where is Prince Lee-Char?"

Anakin stared back at Tamson in silence. Tamson nodded to a Quarren guard who jabbed at the eels with his weapon, causing them to electrocute Kit Fisto and Anakin.

Both Jedi screamed out in agony.

This all became too much for Nossor Ri, who turned his head away.

CHAPTER FIFTEEN

Riff Tamson marched into the Separatist command center and former throne room of the Mon Calamari palace. He had a confident and determined look on his sharklike face. Behind him, Nossor Ri and two armed aqua droids followed.

As they made their way into the center of the large room, a hologram flickered to life. Before them stood a flickering Count Dooku. The aqua droids stood guard on either side as Riff Tamson and Nossor Ri bowed their heads.

"We have captured two Jedi, my lord, as well as the Senator from Naboo," Tamson reported.

"And what of the young Prince?" the Separatist leader asked. It was clear that his patience was running short. "He should have been captured during the first strike. You've now had multiple opportunities to catch him, yet you allow him to slip through your fingers at every turn. Do not make me regret sending you to Mon Cala."

"I have interrogated the Jedi, my lord," Tamson said. "But they will not give up the whereabouts of the Prince. The Jedi's resistance to pain is . . . impressive."

"Press the interrogation, Tamson," Count Dooku ordered. "And I suggest you focus your attention on the Senator from Naboo. I believe you will find that she is the key to breaking young Anakin Skywalker. It is important that you succeed. We cannot allow the Prince to survive. The royal bloodline must be broken."

Nossor Ri swam forward. "Count Dooku, is this necessary?" he pleaded. "The battle is won, the Prince has no army to rally."

"Yet he keeps finding ways to evade you," Dooku added. "I want to see him executed and you're going to make that happen."

"But, my lord, the battle is behind us," Nossor Ri pleaded. "Now is the time for the Quarren to take the lead and think of rebuilding . . ."

"Rebuild?" Dooku snapped back. "While this battle has been won, there is still a war going on,

Nossor Ri. A war in which you pledged your allegiance to the Separatist cause. If you don't wish to live up to your end of our arrangement, I'm sure we can think of other ways to get what we want from Mon Cala. Is that what you'd like for your people?"

"No, my lord," Nossor Ri nervously replied. "It's just that—"

"Do not question me again," Dooku said. "You are standing where you are because I allow it. Your people are alive because I allow it. Do not soon forget it!"

"Of course, Count." Nossor bowed his head and replied, "We owe you everything."

Dooku looked to Tamson, "Have your soldiers arrived?"

Soldiers? Nossor thought. Why would he need to bring in more soldiers?

"Yes, Count, they arrived this morning," Tamson replied. "We now have the city fully under our control."

"Good. Continue as planned," Dooku commanded. The hologram flickered off.

Tamson turned and gestured toward the entrance of the throne room. An army of fierce Karkarodons entered the perimeter of the room, then went through the center. Tamson greeted his soldiers and then led them off into battle.

Nossor Ri shook his lowered head in quiet disappointment. He turned and followed slowly.

Ahsoka and Prince Lee-Char swam through the seaweed and coral tunnels that ran below Mon Calamari City. They needed to find the location of Captain Ackbar.

Lee-Char reckoned that if he had been captured during the last assault, he must have been taken to a Separatist prison camp. Ahsoka was less than sure of this plan.

They continued to search until they found what they had been looking for. In the distance they saw a group of Quarren and aqua droid guards transporting captured Mon Calamari and Gungan soldiers. Prince Lee-Char and Ahsoka swam ahead of the guards and hid among the seaweed. From their hiding spots they watched as the group of prisoners was escorted past them.

"I'm worried about this plan," Ahsoka said. "I'm supposed to keep you safe and this just seems foolish."

"Tell me you've never done anything foolish before," the Prince replied. "Especially when there were so many lives on the line."

Ahsoka knew the Prince was right. She and her Master had charged headstrong into many foolish situations in the past, especially if it meant saving lives.

"Fine," she said. "But at the first sign of danger I'm getting you out of there."

As the prisoners moved past, Ahsoka and Prince Lee-Char rose out from the seaweed and followed behind them. After a short while they came to what they were looking for.

"There it is," Lee-Char said as they came upon an extensive prison refugee camp. It was much larger than the other prisons they had come upon earlier.

The camp consisted of a system of interconnected smaller prisons that made it look like a makeshift village. Around the perimeter, lines of Quarren and aqua droid guards patrolled the exterior area.

"How can we be sure Captain Ackbar's inside?" Ahsoka asked as she tried to see past the guards and into the prison.

"There's only one way to find out," Lee-Char replied.

They waited until they saw another batch of prisoners being escorted by armed aqua droids to the camp. Cautiously, they moved in behind them and then gradually worked their way into the ranks.

Now pretending to be part of the prison group, they followed the guards until they emerged into a large open space.

The Prince was shocked to see the number of Karkarodon soldiers that stood guard around the prisoners.

"That's not a good sign," he said. "It looks like Tamson has brought in his own reinforcements."

"It's only a matter of time before the Quarren find themselves inside the prison as well," Ahsoka added. "The Karkarodon being here might just work in our favor."

One of the prisoners recognized Lee-Char. "Prince, you're a prisoner here as well?" he asked.

Several other Mon Calamari swam over to the Prince. The growing crowd unnerved Ahsoka. She scanned the crowd to see if the guards had noticed. As far as she could tell, they were safe. But she knew that they couldn't stay out in the open like this for long.

"I am here," the Prince began, "but not as a prisoner. I've come with a message. As your future

King, I have not lost hope. The time is coming when you will be free again. I will not fail you."

"We want to believe you," the prisoner said. "But . . . but how can this be possible?"

"Please be patient," the Prince replied. "I have a plan, and when the time comes you will need to be prepared. Let everyone know that we must fight for what is ours."

Suddenly a voice came from behind them. "Commander Tano!"

They turned to see Commander Monnk approaching with two Mon Calamari soldiers.

"Commander! Am I glad to see you," Ahsoka said.

"You both must come with me now," he said as he scanned the area for guards. "You'll attract too much attention here, and I think there's someone who will be happy to see you."

Ahsoka put her hand on the Prince's arm. "Come on, Your Highness," she said. "We have to keep moving."

The Prince seemed reluctant to leave his people, but he had a mission. "Stay safe," he said to them as he turned to leave.

Ahsoka and the Prince followed Commander Monnk as he swam away.

A prisoner called after them. "Prince! You can't leave us here!" he said.

Prince Lee-Char stopped and addressed his people. "Have courage!" he said. "The next time I appear to you, I will appear as your King!"

CHAPTER SIXTEEN

Inside the Separatist prison, Anakin and Kit Fisto remained trapped inside living cages made of giant electric eels. The Jedi struggled, but the cells seemed impossible to escape from. With every motion, the eels sent painful electric shocks through the Jedi.

In his cell, Master Fisto meditated to avoid moving. He was able to calm his mind and remove himself from the horrors of the world around him. Anakin, on the other hand, struggled against the eels. Painful shocks tore through his body. He could not resign himself to being a prisoner while a war raged on around him.

Below them, Padmé and Jar Jar remained trapped in their crablike restraints. Their arms trembled as they worked to steady themselves on the pedestals.

"Anakin, I don't know how much more of this I can take," Padmé said. "It feels like my arms are going to tear out of their sockets."

"Yeah, messa armsa strechen tight," Jar Jar added. "Mesa no likin' dessa pinchy grabby."

Anakin had to find a way to get out of his cage and free the others. He hoped that Ahsoka was having better luck protecting the Prince. He had trained her well, but she often found ways of getting herself into trouble.

"I know it's tough, but you both need to hang on a little longer. Ahsoka's still out there," Anakin said. "Right now, she's our only chance of getting out of here. I'm not having any luck with these eels. I was hoping that they'd run out of electricity, but I don't think that's going to happen."

The doors to the prison opened and Riff Tamson entered with Nossor Ri and a squad of Karkarodon guards in tow.

Tamson swam up to the Jedi and ordered the guard to prod at Anakin's cell.

Anakin screamed as yet another electric charge raced through his body. Tamson laughed. He seemed to take pleasure in watching Anakin suffer.

He swam in closer to the Jedi. His expression

hardened as his eyes locked on Anakin. "I grow tired of waiting, Jedi," he said. "Where is the Prince?"

Kit Fisto opened his eyes and calmly looked to Tamson, who started to swim back and forth in front of their cages.

"Even if we knew, we would not say," Kit Fisto replied.

Tamson sighed. "That's unfortunate." Then he signaled the guards to prod the eels, making them electrocute both of the Jedi.

Both Kit Fisto and Anakin screamed out in agony as electricity tore through their bodies.

Tamson laughed. "To be honest, it matters little to me whether you know the Prince's location or not. I would torture you either way." He swam over to Anakin's cage. "But Count Dooku insists I capture the Prince," he added.

He moved in as close as he could to the cage and fixed his small, dark eyes on Anakin. "And I think there is a slight chance you are deceiving me and holding back some information I could use."

He held his stare for a moment before swimming down to Padmé and Jar Jar.

"And in my position," he continued. "I cannot afford to take chances." He stopped in front of

Padmé and ran his clawed hand down the side of her helmet.

Anakin and Kit Fisto struggled to see what Tamson was doing. Every move set off electric shocks from their cells.

The Karkarodon looked up at the Jedi and smiled. They watched as Tamson rolled his eyes back into his head and opened his massive jaws wide.

"No!" Anakin screamed as he tried to break through his electrified cell.

Tamson's massive jaws crashed down on the glass of Padmé's helmet.

"Ahhhh!" she screamed. "No!"

Padmé watched in terror as the glass cracked around the Karkarodon's mighty teeth. Tamson released his grip. As his teeth pulled away, Padmé could only pray that the glass would hold. Tamson admired the cracked helmet. He appeared satisfied with the result. He looked to Padmé, who was shaken with fear—and then a trickle of water started to creep through the crack in her helmet. It was only a matter of time until her helmet filled with water.

Tamson looked to the two Jedi. "Time is of the essence now," he said. "Tell me what I want to know."

Anakin's eyes grew wide with anger as he struggled against his bonds. Violent shocks of electricity tore through his body. If there were a way to escape these cages, he knew he would find it.

Commander Monnk led Prince Lee-Char, Ahsoka, and the others past the aqua droid guards and into one of the prison's many encampments. There, clones, Gungans, and Mon Calamari prisoners were being held captive. Many were beaten and bruised. Lee-Char watched as his people suffered the indignity of imprisonment. He knew that he had to do something to free them. They pushed farther through the crowd and came upon Meena Tills leaning over an injured Ackbar.

The Senator gave a relieved smile when she saw the Prince. "You're alive!" she said. "Captain, you were right!"

Mon Calamari guards and clone troopers circled Captain Ackbar, keeping a lookout for aqua droids. The others huddled around Ackbar.

"Prince, I knew you would survive the battle," the injured captain said.

"Captain," the Prince replied, "I need your help. I have a plan. I know how we can win this fight.

Both Ackbar and Senator Tills looked at him with curiosity. The battle seemed far from winnable.

"But the battle is over, young Prince," Ackbar said. "And it appears that we have lost."

It pained Ackbar to speak this way to the Prince. He knew that the boy was trying to be a strong leader, but there was just no hope of the Mon Calamari winning this war.

"No," Lee-Char countered. "In truth, we now outnumber our enemy. We can overwhelm them."

"But we are prisoners," Senator Till said. "If we revolted, thousands would die."

"Not if the Quarren struck first and aided in our attack," Lee-Char replied.

"Prince, how can you say this?" Ackbar asked. "The Quarren betrayed us! They assassinated your father!"

"No, Captain," Lee-Char replied. "Riff Tamson murdered my father, of that I am sure."

"The Quarren are being used," Ahsoka added. "I've seen it happen before. Count Dooku has deceived them."

Just then, an aqua droid spotted the group huddled around Ackbar. Using its sensors, it scanned the group and positively identified the Prince.

"I will find Nossor Ri," the Prince said. "He was my father's friend. I know he will listen."

"How can you be certain he will listen?" asked Senator Tills.

"I can't be certain," replied Lee-Char. "But it's time for me to lead, and I feel this is my only course of action."

Everyone went quiet. The Mon Calamari soldiers looked to Ackbar.

"I will ready our people, Prince," Captain Ackbar said.

"But, Captain, you're injured!" Meena Tills said.

Ackbar struggled to his feet. "I'll be ready to fight," he said, turning to Prince Lee-Char, "with our future King."

"I'll marshal the remaining clones and Gungan warriors," Commander Monnk said. "What will your signal be?"

"When a Quarren attacks our enemy," the Prince said, "that will be your sign."

Five aqua droids pushed their way through the crowd trying to get to the Prince. Ahsoka spotted them and went for her lightsaber.

The Prince reached out a hand and stopped her. "No! Stay your blade, my friend," he said.

"You are under arrest," a droid said as they surrounded the Prince.

The Prince rose and faced the aqua droids. "I am Lee-Char, leader of the Mon Calamari people," he said. "And I demand to speak to your superiors!"

The others watched as the Prince confidently stepped forward and gave himself over to the aqua droid guards.

An aqua droid took Ahsoka's two lightsabers and pushed her in line with the Prince. Together, she and Lee-Char were escorted out of the prison camp.

CHAPTER SEVENTEEN

Drop by drop, water trickled into Padmé's helmet. She stood, locked in an unbreakable trap, unable to prevent the water from rising around her head. She was just breaths away from the water level rising above her mouth. The design on the scuba gear prevented her from tilting her head too far backward, but she still struggled. Every tiny bit that she could angle her head gave her a few more minutes of precious life.

Across the chamber, Anakin struggled against his electric bindings. He had been sent by the Jedi Council to be Padmé's protector. Now he stood helpless, trapped in a living cage and unable to break free. Looking to Master Fisto, Anakin saw the elder Jedi meditating in his cell. That was the Jedi way.

From a young age, the Jedi learners were taught to calm the storms of emotion that ran through them. It was said that unchecked emotions like hate and anger could lead the Jedi toward the path of the dark side of the Force.

Still, despite all the training, Anakin could not calm the rage inside him. One of his closest friends was suffering just a few feet away from him and there was nothing he could do.

Tamson circled the Jedi. It was clear that Anakin's feeling for the Senator were strong. Tamson wondered if those feelings were strong enough for the Jedi to betray the location of Prince Lee-Char. The Jedi were supposedly known for their strong resolve, but perhaps, he wondered, they were not so strong-willed after all.

"Your friend's time is running short," Tamson said. "I'm beginning to believe you are both telling the truth and know nothing of the Prince's whereabouts."

"Then do something to save her, Tamson," Anakin said. "There's no point in letting her drown."

"I don't suppose there is," Tamson replied. "Except for the sheer joy of watching it happen.

How often does one have the opportunity to watch a Republic Senator drown right in front of them?"

Anakin lunged at the cage, trying again to break free. "I swear, if she dies, you will pay," he said as electricity soared through him.

Suddenly Tamson's comlink went off. "We have located the Prince and have him in custody," an aqua droid reported. "He has requested an audience with the leadership."

Tamson laughed as he turned from the Jedi. "By all means bring him to me," Tamson replied. "I shall meet you in the throne room."

"Roger, roger," the droid signed off.

Nossor Ri approached Tamson. "The throne room?" he asked.

"Yes," he replied. "I want that little one to see me in my rightful place as ruler of this world."

"Ruler?!" Nossor Ri exclaimed. "That was not our arrangement with Count Dooku!"

The Karkarodon guards restrained Nossor Ri.

"No, it wasn't your arrangement." Tamson laughed. "It was mine!"

Tamson turned and started to swim off.

"Wait!" Anakin called out. "Padmé! You have to save her!"

Tamson slowly turned and watched Padmé's helmet fill with water. "No . . . I don't."

Anakin tried to free himself and go after Tamson, but he was shocked again.

"I am sorry that I'm going to miss it, though," he added. "You'll have to tell me all about it."

Tamson then turned to his guards. "Bring him along," he said. The Karkarodon dragged Nossor Ri out of the room.

"Ani!" Jar Jar called to Anakin. "Meesa have an idea!"

"Not now, Jar Jar!" Anakin snapped. "We need to save Padmé!"

Kit Fisto, who had remained calm, finally spoke. "Anakin, we must create a bubble for her to breathe from. Use the Force to push the water away from her helmet."

"I'm on it," he replied.

Anakin calmed his body and took a few long, slow breaths. In order to use the Force in such a controlled way, he needed to distance himself from the emotions he felt.

He focused his mind only on the water that surrounded Padmé's cracked helmet. He could not think about her terrified face or her cries for help.

He struggled to remove those thoughts from his head. With every heartbeat, the anger and fear he felt faded into the background. Soon they were all but a distant memory.

As his mind cleared of all emotion, he felt the Force move through him and into the water that surrounded Padmé.

Soon, both Jedi reached out with the Force. The water in the room began to slowly swell and then vibrate as the oxygen was ripped from its molecules and reformed as a bubble around Padmé's helmet.

Once the oxygen bubble was large enough to engulf her head, the water in her helmet began to drain out of the crack.

"Isa workin', isa workin'!" Jar Jar cried out.

As the water level lowered, Padmé took several deep breaths. She didn't know how long the Jedi would be able to hold out.

The Jedi continued to concentrate. If their concentration were to be broken, the bubble would collapse and the water would begin flowing back into Padmé's helmet.

Jar Jar noticed something moving from the cage toward Anakin. One of the electric eels moved its head toward Anakin's leg.

"Ani, look out!" Jar Jar called. "Theesa eel-o comin ta bite ya."

But Anakin was too focused on maintaining the air bubble to hear him.

The eel darted its head forward and bit Anakin on the leg. The Jedi broke his concentration, stumbled against the side of the cage, and was electrocuted.

The Force bubble slowly began to collapse around Padmé.

At that moment, Jar Jar started making a noise like a frog. It got louder and louder, until he hacked up a mucus glob and spat it at Padmé.

The spit glob flew and hit Padmé's helmet, coating the cracked glass with a sticky goo. Just then, the bubble created by the Jedi disappeared and the water crashed in on Padmé.

The Jedi looked up and saw that Padmé was still alive, but her helmet was coated in a thick layer of Gungan spit.

Anakin looked at Padmé, covered in Jar Jar's spit. "Padmé! I'm sorry," he said. "I couldn't . . ."

"Isa Gungan waterproofing," Jar Jar said. "Isa why weesa swim so good!"

The two Jedi shared a stunned expression.

Captain Ackbar and Commander Monnk huddled in a secluded corner of the prison camp. Senator Tills stood off to one side, half listening and half pacing.

"They'll certainly kill him," the Senator said. "If they haven't done so already. Captain, I put you in charge of keeping Prince Lee-Char safe and look what happened."

"The Prince knew what he was doing," Ackbar replied. "Whether he succeeds or fails, he will have done it with courage. And that's what defines a leader. The Mon Calamari people will always remember that."

Commander Monnk interrupted. "If the Prince does succeed in his mission, we'll need to be ready," he said. "Captain, are you sure you'll be healthy enough to fight?"

Captain Ackbar gently rubbed at his wounds. "When the time comes, I'll be ready to fight," he said. "Just make sure the rest of the troops are ready."

"I've put the word out to all the imprisoned troops—Mon Calamari, clone, and Gungan—to be prepared to act on a moment's notice," Monnk replied.

"But how will we know when to act if we're all stuck in this prison?" Senator Tills asked.

"When it comes time for Count Dooku to have Prince Lee-Char executed," Captain Ackbar replied, "he'll make sure the whole planet knows."

CHAPTER EIGHTEEN

The doors to the throne room flew open and
a team of Karkarodon guards and aqua droids
escorted the Prince into the room. Behind them,
they dragged in Ahsoka. As she scanned the room,
she made sure to keep an eye on the droid with her
lightsabers. If the Prince's plan didn't work, getting
her weapons back would be their best chance at
escaping.

As they made their way farther into the room,
they saw King Yos Kolina's throne above them,
where days earlier, Prince Lee-Char almost took
his seat as King. Now perched on it, they saw Riff
Tamson. The Karkarodon grinned as he saw the
Prince being led toward him.

Next to Tamson was an uneasy-looking Nossor
Ri. Lee-Char tried to make eye contact with the

Quarren, but Nossor Ri wouldn't look at him. The Prince's whole plan rested on being able to convince the Quarren to join him, but now it seemed doubtful that he could get them to listen.

Lee-Char looked to the other Quarren in the room. Several stood sentry around the room, but on either side of the throne were Karkarodon guards. He feared that they'd rip his throat out if he said the wrong thing.

"Greetings, Prince," Tamson said. "We meet again. I must admit you were more difficult to capture than I anticipated. You have my respect . . . as hunter to his prey."

"I do not seek nor do I want your respect," Prince Lee-Char replied. "I have come to demand the freedom of my people."

"Your people?!" Tamson laughed. "You are mistaken, Prince. They are my people and under my rule. They, like you, are nothing more than slaves."

"Your rule is not recognized here, Tamson! My people are all those who live in these seas, whether they be Mon Calamari or Quarren." Lee-Char looked to Nossor Ri, who momentarily looked up and appeared to take note of what Prince Lee-Char had said.

Tamson shook his head. "Surely you have not come here seeking the aid of Nossor Ri," he said. "Do you really think he would trade his position to join you?"

The Karkarodon guards moved in closer to the Quarren leader. It was clear to Lee-Char that Nossor Ri had no power left. The Quarren were no better off than the Mon Calamari.

"The Quarren are already slaves!" the Prince replied. "Though they may not see it. Nossor Ri, you knew my father. Whatever differences our people had in the past, surely you must know we can work together to make Mon Cala whole. Dooku and Tamson want only to exploit us and leave our cities broken and our resources depleted. What will then be left for the Quarren?"

Nossor Ri kept his head lowered.

"Well, Nossor Ri, would you like to join this pitiful little fish and his dead father?" Tamson asked.

The Karkarodon guards laughed as Nossor Ri sat down without saying a word.

"There, you see? Ha!" Tamson went on. "What good would their help be, anyway, Prince? The Quarren are more gutless than your people."

The Quarren guards exchanged glances as the

Karkarodon's gurgled laughter filled the throne room.

Prince Lee-Char stood tall. "As long as I live, I shall give all people of Mon Cala hope to fight another day."

"Hmmm. Hope," Tamson said. "We are of the same mind, Prince. That is why I have scheduled your public execution. Take him away!"

"You will not get away with this. The people of Mon Cala will rise up and you will not be able to stop us," the Prince said as the guards grabbed him by the shoulders. "Nossor Ri!" Lee-Char called back. "There's still time! Unite and we will defend our home."

Tamson continued to laugh as the aqua droids dragged the Prince from the throne room.

"I don't think it worked," Lee-Char said to Ahsoka. "Nossor Ri wouldn't even look at me. Without his support, we're doomed."

"I'm not going to let them execute you," Ahsoka said. "If the Quarren don't come to your aid, I'll do what I can to free you."

"Thank you, Ahsoka," he said. "You've become a trusted friend, but if that is my fate, then that is what must happen."

"Your death will not help anything, Prince," she replied. "I swore that I'd keep you safe and that's what I intend to do."

Anakin, Kit Fisto, Padmé, and Jar Jar remained imprisoned inside the Senate chambers. Calmly standing in his electrified cage, Anakin focused on his meditation.

"All right, I think I'm getting the hang of this," he said, then was instantly shocked again.

Kit Fisto laughed. "Less talking helps."

Four Karkarodon guards entered and took hold of the cages. They turned and swam them up out of the Senate. A group of aqua droids grabbed Padmé and Jar Jar in their restraints and followed behind. The movement of the eel cages caused the Jedi to be electrocuted.

"Jar Jar, I can't see anything," Padmé said, blinded by the Gungan phlegm on her helmet. "Where are they taking us?"

"Hey, yousa!" Jar Jar called to one of the aqua droids. "Where yousa taking us?"

"To the execution of Prince Lee-Char," the droid replied.

A crowd of prisoners had been assembled inside the throne room. Commander Monnk and Senator Tills stood with a still-wounded Captain Ackbar. Around them, aqua droids and Quarren soldiers stood guard while Trident drill ships patrolled the outside area.

At the center of the gathering, a group of ferocious Karkarodon circled Prince Lee-Char.

The Mon Calamari throne had been placed at the head of the gathering. And in it sat Riff Tamson. To his right stood an uncomfortable Nossor Ri, who was flanked by Karkarodon guards. Still in their bindings, Anakin, Kit Fisto, Padmé, and Jar Jar were placed behind the throne.

Anakin watched as Ahsoka was guided over to them by two hulking Karkarodon guards.

"Good job protecting the Prince," he said to her.

"It's all part of the plan," she replied.

"I was hoping you were going to say that," Anakin added with a wry smile. "Anything I can do?"

"Unfortunately, this time it's out of our hands," she replied. "It's all on the Prince."

"I'm not sure I like this plan after all," Anakin said to her.

Riff Tamson signaled to a guard, and Prince Lee-Char was led out in front of the throne. A group of about a dozen Quarren guards stood to the right of the throne, near Nossor Ri.

Riff Tamson addressed Prince Lee-Char. "For crimes against the Separatist state, I command the execution of former Prince, Lee-Char."

"Is this part of your plan?" Anakin asked Ahsoka. "Because if it is, I'm liking it even less."

"I never said that it was the best plan, Master," she said. "But I've learned everything that I know from you."

"That does not make me feel any better," Anakin replied.

"You have no authority to execute a head of state," Padmé called out. "Mon Cala is still a Republic world and therefore you must obey its laws."

Tamson ignored the Senator and nodded to the guards that surrounded the Prince. "You have your orders."

Two Karkarodon guards swam up to Lee-Char and flexed their jaws. They were planning on devouring the Prince in front of everyone. In the crowd, Ackbar and Commander Monnk looked at each other as if waiting for some signal.

A Quarren guard spotted Ackbar and pushed his way through the crowd. Ackbar turned to see several Quarren guards approaching him and Commander Monnk. "Captain," the guard said. "Nossor Ri and the Quarren are with you."

The Quarren guard handed Ackbar a weapon. They nodded at each other as they headed toward the Prince. Another Quarren guard handed a weapon to Commander Monnk, who moved in behind Ackbar.

Riff Tamson grew impatient and yelled to the Karkarodon circling the Prince.

"Kill HIM!"

CHAPTER NINETEEN

The Karkarodon guards reared their heads back at Tamson's command to kill the Prince.

The Mon Calamari prisoners screamed as they watched the guards lunge at their leader.

Captain Ackbar stood calmly with his blaster hidden from view. His eyes were fixed on Nossor Ri. The fate of the Mon Calamari was in the hands of the Quarren, and he hoped that they would not let the Prince down.

From where he was, he could probably get two blasts off before the guards would be on him. If the Quarren didn't do something soon, it would be up to him and Commander Monnk to save the Prince.

Ahsoka took a deep breath. She would have just one chance to free the Prince. She would have to escape from the aqua droid's restraints, retrieve her lightsabers, and take out the Karkarodon guards before they could turn on her.

She looked quickly to Anakin who could sense what she was about to do. She gave him a knowing nod and then briefly closed her eyes.

With the aqua droid holding her lightsabers in sight, Ahsoka concentrated all her energy on breaking free of the guard's grip.

Before she could break free, the squidlike Nossor Ri leaped forward and quite unexpectedly squirted a black, inklike substance in the water around the execution area. The biological ability to release a dark pigment into the water was a defense mechanism that all Quarren possessed. Dating back to the early days of the Quarren race, they used this as a smokescreen to escape from predators. As the Quarren evolved, they became less reliant on the use of their ink sacs, and it was something rarely seen by other species.

Following Nossor Ri's lead, the Quarren guards near the throne released their ink into the water. Soon, the throne and Lee-Char were consumed in a cloud of thick, black ink.

Captian Ackbar nodded to Commander Monnk and they quickly blasted the aqua droid guards around them. The Quarren soldiers followed suit.

Tamson roared through the darkness as he lost sight of the Prince. "Kill him," he hollered. "I want him dead. I want all of them dead!"

Through the ink cloud, Nossor Ri grabbed the Prince and pulled him out of danger. "Come with me," he said. "I'll get you to safety."

The massive, sharklike Karkarodons raged through the murk to find their target.

Tamson emerged from the ink cloud to see that the Quarren guard had freed the prisoners. A combined army of Mon Calamari, Quarren, clones, and Gungans were charging the throne.

"You have made a huge mistake, Nossor Ri," he screamed as he scanned the room for the Prince. "I will take great pleasure in devouring you myself."

As the remaining ink cloud dispersed, Ahsoka watched as Ackbar and Prince Lee-Char fought alongside the Quarren. She looked to Anakin, who gave her a knowing nod.

"Hold on, Master," she said. "I'll have you free in no time."

She focused on the aqua droid that had been restraining her and then flipped up, out of its grasp. In the air, she knocked back the droids around her and landed. Then she spotted the aqua droid that held her two lightsabers. Using the Force, she pulled them both to her. Before the droid knew what happened, Ahsoka ignited one of the blades and cut the droid down.

Ahsoka quickly freed Anakin and Kit Fisto by cutting through their eel cages. Kit Fisto moved to release Jar Jar and Padmé as Ahsoka tossed Anakin one of her lightsabers.

"It took you long enough, Snips," Anakin said. "Now let's see if we can't even the score."

Anakin ignited the green blade and together he and his Padawan stormed into the heart of the fray. Around them, the Quarren soldiers armed the clones and Gungans with weapons. The combined army greatly outnumbered the aqua droids who were being pushed back.

Tamson continued to search for the Prince. He watched as aqua droids fell one by one at the hands of the Mon Calamari and Quarren. His Karkarodon soldiers were the only thing holding back the advancing forces.

"Send in more droids," Tamson yelled to one of the aqua droids by his side. "Call in all the reserves. I don't want anything in this room left alive."

"Roger, roger," an aqua droid replied as it radioed for more reinforcements.

Tamson continued to scan the battle for signs of the Prince.

Off to the side, Prince Lee-Char stood with Nossor Ri.

"Thank you for what you did in there," Lee-Char said. "Without Quarren support, Mon Cala would be no more."

"I can't believe things got this far out of hand," Nossor Ri said. "I'm so sorry. Your father was a great leader and I should have trusted that you would do the same. Under my leadership, I handed our planet over to the Separatists. I was a fool."

"It is true that your quest for power was misguided, but you were also betrayed by those you trusted," the Prince said. "But we have a chance to make things right. There's a battle unfolding in front of us, and I plan on leading our people to victory."

Lee-Char extended his hand to the Quarren.

Nossor Ri accepted the Prince's hand. "You are more like your father than I gave you credit for," he said. "I would be honored to follow you into battle."

Prince Lee-Char rose and charged into the center of the fight. Through the fighting, he saw Tamson heading his way. "Look out!" he called to the others. It was too late. The massive Karkarodon ripped through all the Mon Calamari and Quarren soldiers that stood between him and the Prince.

Prince Lee-Char and Tamson stood head-to-head. The Karkarodon swung a powerful claw at the Prince, who did his best to fend off the attack. Tamson easily outpowered the young Lee-Char, but the Prince wouldn't give up.

The fighting around them slowed, and all eyes fell upon their struggle. The Mon Calamari and Quarren both cheered their Prince on.

The Prince, despite his willpower, could not hold out much longer. He made one final lunge at Tamson. Lee-Char attempted to grab a hold of him but the Karkarodon swatted him away.

"You've lost, Prince." He laughed as he bared his teeth for one final assault. "This planet is mine now. And there's nothing that you or those squids can do to stop me."

A battered Lee-Char rose from the floor and held up a thermal detonator that he'd pulled from Tamson's belt during his last attack.

Tamson didn't even flinch. "Do you even know how to turn it on?" he asked the young Prince.

Without a second thought, Lee-Char threw the thermal detonator at Tamson and shot it with his blaster.

A massive explosion rocked the throne room. As the smoke cleared, Lee-Char searched through the rubble for signs of Tamson. Then, he saw his opponent. He swam forward and saw Tamson's lifeless body floating to the floor.

The Prince was immediately surrounded by Mon Calamari and Quarren soldiers. Captain Ackbar pushed through and made his way up to Lee-Char.

"Are you okay, Your Highness?" Ackbar asked.

"I think so, Captain," Lee-Char replied.

"Good," Ackbar replied. "Because we still have a war to win."

Around them, the remaining Karkarodon soldiers and aqua droids moved in. The united Mon Calamari and Quarren Army, along with the clones and Gungans under Prince Lee-Char's command, continued the fight.

Soon the Karkarodon soldiers realized the battle was lost and fled the throne room. The remaining aqua droids stood alone in the chamber. They were vastly outnumbered. Within seconds, they were no more.

Nossor Ri swam to the Prince's side. "The day is won!" he called out.

"Long live the Prince!" Ackbar cheered as the united Mon Cala Army gathered around the Prince. Soon the whole room was chanting along with Captain Ackbar.

CHAPTER TWENTY

The throne room had been somewhat rebuilt, and everyone—Quarren and Mon Calamari—assembled neatly on either side of a wide aisle.

Lee-Char emerged and made his way before the room. Senator Meena Tills and Nossor Ri stood at the other end of the aisle along with a Mon Calamari holy man. Behind them stood Padmé, Captain Ackbar, and Jar Jar Binks, along with the Jedi. Ahsoka smiled proudly at the Prince.

Lee-Char swam purposefully down the aisle, meeting the eyes of his subjects. He nodded and smiled confidently as he went.

When Prince Lee-Char reached the front of the aisle, Senator Tills stepped forward. "Your father would be so proud," she said.

"I know," the Prince replied.

The holy man stepped forward and addressed Lee-Char. "May the blessings of the water keep you, the might of your ancestors give you strength," he said.

Nossor Ri then swam forward with the crown of Mon Cala.

"As representative of the Quarren people," he said, "I pledge our loyalty to you."

"And as your King, I pledge my loyalty to all the people of Mon Cala," Lee-Char announced to the room.

Nossor Ri nodded and placed the crown on Lee-Char's head.

The holy man turned to face the room. "I present King Lee-Char!" he announced.

Everyone in the room cheered. "Long live the King! Long live King Lee-Char!"